People Who Have Helped

SOJOURNER TRUTH

by Susan Taylor-Boyd

Picture Credits
The Bettmann Archive, 18, 31; Sharon Burris © Gareth Stevens, Inc., 1989, 20; Historical Pictures Service, Chicago, 10, 26, 35, 42, 59; Library of Congress, 14, 16, 22, 43 (both); Courtesy of the Louisiana State Museum, 6; Bernice B. Lowe Collection, Michigan Historical Collections, Bentley Historical Library, University of Michigan, 4, 13 (bottom), 27, 28, 32, 33, 38, 51; Milwaukee County Historical Society, 9, 13 (top), 29, 30, 37; Missouri Historical Society, 25, 45; Courtesy of the New York Historical Society, New York City, 24 (top and bottom), 41, 49; © Harry J. Quinn, 1989, cover; Schomburg Center for Research in Black Culture, The New York Public Library, Astor, Lenox and Tilden Foundations, 11; UPI/Bettmann Newsphotos, 53, 55, 56, 57.

North American paperback edition first published in 1990 by **Morehouse Publishing**

Corporate Office
P.O. Box 1321
Harrisburg, Pennsylvania 17105

Editorial Office
78 Danbury Road
Wilton, Connecticut 06897

Library of Congress Cataloging-in-Publication Data

Taylor-Boyd, Susan, 1949-
    Sojourner Truth / by Susan Taylor-Boyd.
      p. cm. — (People who have helped the world)
    Summary: Follows the life of the former slave who gained renown as an abolitionist and advocate of women's rights.
    Includes index.
    ISBN 0-8368-0101-6
    1. Truth, Sojourner, d. 1883—Juvenile literature. 2. Afro-Americans—Biography—Juvenile literature. 3. Abolitionists—United States—Biography—Juvenile literature. 4. Social reformers—United States—Biography—Juvenile literature. [1. Truth, Sojourner, d. 1883. 2. Afro-Americans—Biography. 3. Abolitionists. 4. Reformers.] I. Title. II. Series.
E185.97.T8T38   1989   305.5'67'0924—dc19   [B]   [92]   89-4345

Gareth Stevens ISBN 0-8368-0101-6 (lib. bdg.)
Morehouse ISBN 0-8192-1541-4 (softcover)

Series conceived by Helen Exley
Series editor: Rhoda Irene Sherwood
Editor: Valerie Weber
Editorial assistant: Scott Enk
Layout: Kristi Ludwig
Picture research: Daniel Helminak
Research assistant: Kathleen Weisfeld Barrilleaux

SOJOURNER TRUTH

The courageous former slave whose eloquence helped promote human equality

by Susan Taylor-Boyd

MOREHOUSE PUBLISHING

Harrisburg, PA   Wilton, CT

Raising her voice for equality

"I want to ride. I want to ride! I want to ride!" The white passengers on the Washington, D.C., streetcar turned to see a tall, elderly black woman running after the car, shaking her cane and shouting at the conductor. It was 1867, after the Emancipation Proclamation had freed the slaves in the southern United States and after the Civil War. Streetcars in the nation's capital were supposed to be integrated.

Yet laws don't always change the way people think. The conductors often refused to stop for African-Americans. But this black woman, Sojourner Truth, had been demanding all her life to ride with the rest of humanity. She called for blacks to be freed from slavery, she demanded that all women be considered equal to men, she expected everyone in the nation to have all the rights of citizenship. Now this streetcar refused to stop because she was black. She'd have none of that.

Running as fast as she could, she caught up to the car and jumped aboard with the white passengers at the next stop.

"Get out of the way and let this lady through," the conductor snapped at Sojourner, pulling her aside as a white woman climbed the steps.

"I'm a lady, too!" Truth shouted and took a seat. She had dedicated her life to winning little victories like this. No one would deny her.

This illiterate black woman overcame her inability to read and write, using instead her quick mind, her powerful voice, and her dominating six-foot (2-m) stature to demand that a nation of slaveholders and white males accept blacks and women as equal partners in the U.S. government and economy. While she lived to witness the emancipation of the slaves and the enactment of the Thirteenth, Fourteenth, and

Opposite: This engraving of Sojourner Truth as a young woman was created from the artist's imagination. As a young slave, Truth would not have been important or wealthy enough to have an engraving done of her.

Fifteenth Amendments, she knew even more would need to be done. "I go for agitating," she proclaimed. And the agitation she set in motion persisted into the twentieth century with the work of civil rights activists and women's rights advocates.

Amazingly, such an outspoken woman came from an oppressed background. Sojourner Truth was born a slave.

"Slaves, horses, and other cattle . . ."

In 1799, New York State passed a decree granting freedom to male slaves born after July 4 in that year once they reached age twenty-eight. Female slaves had to serve their masters until age twenty-five.

But Truth never had the luck of easy solutions.

She was born Isabella Hardenbergh in Ulster County, New York, in 1797, two years too early for this guaranteed freedom. Isabella, or Belle as she was called, was the eleventh child of Mau-Mau Bett, a woman of strong religious convictions. From her mother, Belle learned the faith that would give her the strength and courage needed for her battles. "My good Master kept me," she would say, "for he had something for me to do."

This painting shows a Southern plantation that was about ten times bigger than the Northern farms that Truth worked on. Fewer slaves were needed on a small farm than on a large plantation, so farm slaves usually stayed in the owner's basement while plantation slaves usually lived in shacks, away from the main house.

But in the eyes of New York, she had another master, Colonel Charles Hardenbergh. Belle carried his name because, as property, slaves had to take the name of their masters.

Evenings in the mildewed cellar of the Hardenbergh house where Belle's family lived, Mau-Mau would gather her children to tell them about hope. "My children there is a God, who hears and sees you. When you are beaten, or cruelly treated, or fall into any trouble, you must ask help of him, and he will always hear and help you." Belle looked at her mother, "Who is God, anyhow, mammy?" "Why child," Mau-Mau answered, "it's him that made all them." And she pointed to the stars.

At first, Belle did not think much about God. She was too busy being a child. But in time, her hardships increased, and she remembered the faith in God that Mau-Mau had, even when her mother's life seemed horrible. Belle began to have daily conversations with God, and she would ask him to help her and to guide her. She would always listen for God's reply. He would not always answer immediately, but she trusted that in time "the Lord," as she addressed God, would give her a word or a sign. At every major turning point in her life, Belle would stop and ask God's advice.

Belle became a kitchen slave to Mrs. Hardenbergh. She was a headstrong child, and as she grew tall, she also grew obstinate. Neither of these were good qualities for a kitchen slave who had to serve the owners directly and bend over a kitchen fire. So Mrs. Hardenbergh declared she would have to be sold.

Belle's father, Baumfree, offered himself in her place. But Baumfree was already old and crippled by the time Belle was born. Hardenbergh could not make enough profit from Baumfree to justify keeping an insolent slave girl. So Belle went on the auction block.

"Slaves, horses, and other cattle will be sold," read the notice. But no one wanted her. She stood staring at the sky, looking every bit a lazy and undisciplined girl. Finally, frustrated, Hardenbergh cried out, "I'll throw in a flock of sheep if you'll buy this girl."

"One hundred dollars," cried out John Neely. And Belle was sold for the first of many times. She was nine years old.

"The purchase of a Negro was usually to secure a wife desired by one of his men or to get a specially skilled blacksmith or carpenter. It was always to add to the industrial efficiency of the plantation rather than to acquire a large number of slaves."
Nellie Thomas McColl, remembering her grandfather's plantation

An orphaned child

Leaving her mother and father caused Belle great agony. She knew that it would be a miracle if she ever saw her parents again. Although Neely's farm was only a few miles away from the Hardenberghs, slaves were not given many days off to go visiting. After all, if slaves didn't work day and night for their masters, how could the slaves make a profit for them? Belle would see her parents again only three times before their deaths.

When Hardenbergh sold Belle, he also gave Baumfree and Mau-Mau their freedom. But these slaves had known only one life and one home — the dark, crowded cellar of the Hardenberghs where all the slaves lived together. So they chose to remain and continue working for Hardenbergh in exchange for bed and board.

Disease spread easily among the slaves in the damp cellar. Mau-Mau was often ill. The dampness also led to palsy, tremors of the body, that crippled both Mau-Mau and Baumfree.

While her parents struggled to survive in their cellar, Belle faced great difficulties of her own. Because Hardenbergh was Dutch, Belle spoke only low Dutch, a dialect spoken by working-class Dutch people. But her new master was an Englishman. Neely hated the fact that Belle could not understand him when he ordered her about. He thought she was acting stupid on purpose. His solution was to whip her until her flesh bled.

The scars remained with Belle forever. Later, she told an audience at a women's rights convention, "When I hear them tell of whipping women on the bare flesh, it makes my flesh crawl! . . . Oh, my God, what a way is this of treating human beings?"

Once Belle learned English, Neely saw that she was bright indeed and as strong as any boy. So Neely decided to sell her quickly, before she became sick and weak, in order to make a profit on her. Martin Schryver, a fisherman who also ran a tavern, bought her to help out with his customers. Schryver treated Belle well, but when a buyer offered three hundred dollars for her, Schryver agreed. At thirteen, she became the slave of John Dumont.

A small victory

Belle's years with Dumont would be her most significant years in slavery. Dumont treated his slaves with all the consideration he did his animals. Even this treatment was kinder than that given to many slaves at that time.

Once again Belle became a kitchen slave. An incident at this time fortified her faith that God "shields the innocent, and causes them to triumph over their enemies," as she would later say. She would draw on this faith to support her future battle for freedom and equality.

Mrs. Dumont's white servant, Kate, did not like Belle because the young black girl was so capable in the kitchen. So Kate set out to get Belle in trouble. Each day Belle would boil potatoes and each day the potatoes would turn black. No matter how carefully she washed and boiled them, they would come from the water black and inedible. For her error, John Dumont would beat Belle.

But in every other matter, he was pleased with Belle. So the family was confused by her continued failure with the potatoes. One day, the Dumonts' daughter, Gertrude, caught Kate throwing ashes into the potato pot. The mystery was solved! Gertrude ran to tell her father, and Kate was punished. It was a small vindication for Belle. For the first time, but certainly not the last, a white person's injustice to her had been surmounted — in this case, thanks to someone who cared about justice.

True love and a forced marriage

Another significant event for Belle was her courtship with Bob, a slave from a neighboring farm. Belle and Bob were very much in love, and when Belle became ill one day, Bob risked punishment to visit her. But just as he reached Dumont's yard, a man named Catlin, Bob's master, and his sons caught up with him.

From her cellar window, Belle heard Catlin scream, "Knock down the black rascal," as he repeatedly struck Bob with the heavy end of his cane. The beating continued until Bob crumpled to the ground, mangled and bloody. John Dumont heard the commotion and ran out as Catlin raised his cane yet

Children orphaned by the Civil War. Black families were torn apart by both slavery and the war to abolish it. Many whites considered blacks savages who had no family love. The slave owners used this belief to justify selling away the slaves' family members. The owners believed that any grief the slaves felt would be quickly forgotten.

Some white owners and overseers considered slaves part of their livestock. They felt that slaves could not be reasoned with but had to be beaten and punished as if they were stubborn, untrainable animals. These owners believed that "feeling the lash" would make the slaves more subservient.

again. "I'll have no niggers* killed here," Dumont shouted. So Catlin took a rope, tied Bob to his wagon, and took him back to his farm. Dumont followed to be sure that no further harm would come to Bob.

That was the last Belle saw of her love. Within a few days, Catlin married Bob to one of his slave girls. A few years later, Bob died.

Soon Belle was married to Thomas, an elderly slave of the Dumonts. Thomas had been married twice before, but Dumont had sold both his wives. Soon Belle had a baby, Diana, who was followed by Elizabeth, Peter, Sophia, and a girl who, it is believed, died in infancy. Peter was named after her brother, whom the Hardenberghs had sold when he was five. Later her son Peter would figure in another of Belle's significant experiences.

Mau-Mau and Baumfree die

Mau-Mau Bett died before the birth of Belle's first child. The damp cellar had aggravated a leg sore that would not heal, and the fever from the infection had made her weak. One day, Baumfree found Mau-Mau face down in the mud of the cellar. She had fallen in a palsy fit and had been too weak to get up. A few hours after Baumfree put her in her bed, she died.

Baumfree had lost his companion and his strength. "Oh," he cried at her funeral, "I had thought God would take me first!" After Mau-Mau's death, since Baumfree was too old and blind to be of any use to them, the Hardenberghs gave him a cabin in the woods.

When Diana was born, Belle wrapped her snugly and began a twelve-mile (19-km) walk to the Hardenberghs. When she finally arrived, she was told her father was now in a cabin on his own twenty miles (32 km) up the road. Belle was heartbroken. Too tired to go on, she returned to the Dumont farm.

---

*People of this time, even Sojourner Truth in her speeches, commonly referred to blacks or African-Americans as "niggers." While this is no longer an acceptable term, the author and editor wish to be historically correct in their use of the language. Please see the glossary for a further discussion of terms referring to race.

Abolitionist leaders waged their moral battle through private newspapers, pamphlets, and letters. In 1835, President Andrew Jackson asked the U.S. Congress to pass laws prohibiting abolitionists from circulating their literature in the South. The postmaster of New York had already censored any abolitionist literature going out of New York State. They feared the writings would incite the slaves to revolt.

She never saw her father again. That winter, too weak to care for himself, he died of starvation and exposure. Later, in her battles to free all slaves, Belle would note that she had learned from Baumfree's last years that freedom can also bring great pain.

The abolitionists

In the Northern states, a group of people who opposed slavery and worked to abolish it had begun to gain political power. Called abolitionists, these people urged the Northern states to abolish slavery. With the inventions of the Industrial Revolution, farming no longer required huge work forces, and in the cities, new factories needed workers. It made sense, the abolitionists argued, to free the slaves and to encourage them to take low-paying factory jobs.

The abolitionists also appealed to the religious consciences of Northerners. In fact, abolitionism had begun as a religious movement. Many of the abolitionist leaders were itinerant preachers in the North. They would arrive in a town, put up a tent, and advertise their meetings, called revivals. Their message stated that people were morally obligated by the Bible to end sinful practices, and one sinful practice needing immediate attention was slavery. In God's eyes, they said, all people were equal. By the 1830s, these revivalist meetings had become political meetings where men and women argued for an end to slavery.

"Our nation will yet be obliged to pay sigh for sigh, groan for groan, and dollar for dollar, to this wronged and outraged race."
Parker Pillsbury, abolitionist

11

It was the religious appeal that first attracted Belle's interest. For some time, she had believed, remarkably, that slavery was right and just, that God had instituted slavery for a reason. But as she prayed more, as she watched slaves being mistreated, as she heard more of the abolitionist speeches, she became convinced that slavery was not the work of God. "I knew slavery was a curse. I had been a slave and a chattel, and I went to work then [against slavery]."

Later she would challenge an audience with the words, "Children, who made your skin white? Was it not God? Who made mine black? Was it not the same God? Now children . . . get rid of your prejudice and learn to love colored children, that you may be all the children of your Father in Heaven."

The work of the abolitionists led to a new law in New York. Now all slaves, even those born before 1799, would be given their freedom on July 4, 1827. Belle could not believe her good fortune. She began to prepare for her freedom.

Then an even more fantastic promise came her way! John Dumont told her, "You have worked so hard that I'll give your freedom to you one year early." Belle's spirit filled with joy.

As 1826 began, Belle looked forward to the summer. Then early in the year, during the winter harvest, Belle sliced her hand with a scythe. Despite the pain, she kept working, knowing that in a few short months she would be free. On July 4, Dumont came to her, saying, "You can't have your freedom. You didn't do as much work as usual these past months."

Flight to freedom

Belle was aghast at what she had heard! Dumont had broken his promise to her. The thought of another year of enslavement was unbearable. She gathered her children together and told them they would be staying with their father for a time while she went to find work as a free woman. Only her baby, Sophia, would accompany her. Leaving before dawn, Belle began her journey to freedom — a journey that would last a lifetime.

Belle went straight to the home of Isaac and Maria Van Wagener, a Quaker family opposed to slavery.

She knew that in a few hours, Dumont would come looking for his escaped slave, so she had to find a refuge. The Van Wageners listened to her story of Dumont's unfulfilled promise. They agreed that Belle deserved her freedom. First of all, they believed slavery was morally wrong. But more important, they believed Dumont had broken his word.

As she feared, Dumont soon caught up with her.

"You ran away, Belle," he said.

"No," she replied. "I took the freedom you promised me."

Although the Van Wageners did not condone slavery, they knew that Dumont would not give up Belle unless he had some compensation. So they paid Dumont twenty-five dollars for Belle and her baby.

Belle fell at Isaac Van Wagener's feet and cried, "Thank you, master!"

"Don't call me that," he said, looking at Belle gently. "You have no master but God."

Now Belle understood what freedom meant. She might be poor and she might be illiterate, but with God's guidance and strength, she felt she would be in control of her life.

A great light

When she was thirty years old, Belle had one encounter with God that gave her an even stronger faith. She had always prayed to God daily. She called these prayers her "little talks."

Above: Quakers did not believe in violence. But they were often the victims of violent acts from people who did not want them to protect slaves.

Below: Truth wanted people to know about her experiences, but she could not write. So friends helped her keep records.

March 1ᵗʰ 1832 .... Isabella Van Wagn... rience .... It is now five years this ...ter since I knew there was a risen ...viour.

But during one of these talks in 1827, Belle became aware of a great light surrounding her. "Who are you?" she wondered. Even as she asked the question, she knew it was Jesus. Five years later she had a friend write on a scrap of paper the date she said she first met Jesus Christ.

Although this experience was meaningful, Belle believed that God the Father had more power than Jesus did. She continued to pray directly to God and to depend on God's guidance and help throughout her life. She would need that help very soon.

"I'll have my son back!"

Dumont had sold Belle's son, Peter, to a neighbor, Solomon Gedney. Belle had not been very concerned because she knew that according to New York state law, Gedney would be forced to give Peter his freedom on July 4, 1827. She also knew that New York state law forbade any slave owner to trade a slave out of state, so Peter would remain close by until he was freed. But despite the law, Solomon Gedney traded Peter to his brother-in-law in Alabama.

Cotton was a profitable crop for Southern plantations, but growing it required a huge work force to plant, tend, and pick the crop. So slave labor was important to Southern plantation owners. Because of laws against importing new slaves, plantation owners bought or kidnapped Northern blacks to work their fields.

Immediately, Belle rushed to the Dumont farm. "Missus," she asked Mrs. Dumont, "have you been and sent my son away down to Alabama? How could you do it?"

"What a fuss you make about a little nigger!" Mrs. Dumont laughed.

Belle looked at her former mistress with determination. "I'll have my son back!"

"How? You have no money — nothing."

Belle turned to leave and then shot back, "God will help me." Later, remembering this moment, she said, "I felt as if the power of a nation was within me."

Driven by her sense that injustice was being done, Belle hurried to the courthouse in Kingston, New York, and convinced a lawyer to draw up a legal paper demanding that Solomon Gedney appear in court. In doing so, she became one of the first black people ever to fight a white person in court in a country long governed by laws favoring whites over blacks.

Gedney could not ignore the law any longer. He immediately went to Alabama and brought Peter back with him.

But Gedney argued that Peter still belonged to him. Belle would have to go to court if she was to ever have her son back with her. Her lawyer did not press the case, and no court date was established. Instead, he told Belle to be patient.

Belle knew that patience for a black person in those days meant waiting for nothing. She had to act. She had to take charge of her life. In two days, she had a new lawyer, and twenty-four hours later, Gedney, Peter, and Belle were before a judge.

Belle's day in court

Belle was nervous about meeting Gedney in court. She knew that being black and female gave her little power. But she had no other option. She would have to trust God and the judge.

Peter entered the courtroom without looking up. Clutching Gedney's legs in terror, Peter refused to go to Belle. "She is not my mother. I want to stay with my master," he insisted. Belle thought she had lost her son forever, but the judge was not convinced. The questions began.

"How did you get that scar on your forehead, son?"
"A horse kicked me."
"And the other scars?"

Peter began to sob. The judge suspected that Gedney had forced the child to lie. Taking the boy aside, the judge questioned him. Then he ordered that Peter be given to Belle. She had won her son. She had beaten a white man. Now she knew that she had to be strong and fight for all the rights owed her as a member of the human race.

The Kingdom

Once Belle had won Peter back, she returned to Dumont and asked that he care for her remaining three daughters. But she still had to support Peter, Sophia, and herself. Work on farms was too hard and too scarce. Most jobs were filled by slaves, and the other jobs paid too little.

So in 1829, Belle decided to take her family to New York City. Through the Van Wageners, Belle learned of a religious family, the Piersons, who would hire her to do housework.

Elijah Pierson was a wealthy widower who was convinced that God would establish a kingdom of love and peace on earth. Pierson had told Belle of a prophet who would come and show them the way to this new kingdom. Belle had seen pictures of Jesus with long hair and a beard, and when Pierson spoke of the prophet, he also spoke of Jesus.

So when a long-haired, bearded man came to the Piersons' door and told Belle, "My name is Matthias, and I have been sent by God to set up the kingdom of heaven on earth," she believed him. With Pierson's wealthy friends and Belle's willing assistance, Matthias set up a church on a country estate in Sing Sing, New York, that they called The Kingdom.

But Matthias was soon revealed to be both lazy and impious. Quarrels broke out among the followers. Depressed by the failure of The Kingdom, Belle realized that love and peace were goals that people had to work hard to achieve. They did not just rain down from heaven.

She also learned that saying she was equal didn't mean that she would be treated equally. As the only black member of The Kingdom, Belle did most of the work. While she had expected that these white people who spoke of love would treat her with respect and as an equal, she discovered that they were not so unlike her previous masters.

When Elijah Pierson died, Belle learned all too quickly how capable her white friends were of turning against her.

Another lawsuit

One of The Kingdom's couples, the Folgers, accused Belle not only of being responsible for Pierson's death, but of trying to poison them as well! But Belle was devoted to Pierson and had nursed him faithfully through his illnesses. She knew that if she gave in to the Folgers' threats, she would never again be a free woman. In fact, she would certainly die in jail.

So with the same stubbornness and strength she had drawn on to save Peter, she determined to save herself. She hired a lawyer, sued the Folgers for slander, and won a cash settlement. Once again, by trusting God and the court and by standing up for her

In the 1840s, New York City grew rapidly. Merchants, builders, doctors, and lawyers got rich serving the expanding population. Many of the European immigrants lived in slums, while blacks who worked as servants and housemaids earned enough money to stay out of the slums. Social reformers tried to establish shelters and food banks for the poor, but most citizens simply ignored the poverty.

rights, Belle had achieved success against great odds. With her money, she left The Kingdom and returned to New York City.

The ugly city

Belle knew her money would not last very long, and with Pierson dead, she had no employer. She had to find work again as a household servant to a wealthy white family.

Worse, Peter had become involved in many illegal activities and with the unsavory people who pursued these activities. Belle knew that Peter's beatings when he was in Alabama with Solomon Gedney had left him angry and confused, but her own legal struggles had not given her time to attend to Peter's emotional needs. Every year he became more and more undisciplined.

Finally Belle had to throw him out of her employer's house. It grieved her greatly because she'd already lost her brother, Peter, when he had been sold away. And now her son, Peter's namesake, at only fourteen, was gone.

Peter was soon arrested and thrown in prison. A friend of his, a barber, interceded with the authorities. He promised to find Peter a place on the crew of a whaling ship. Belle was delighted. Now Peter would be out of the city and away from all its terrible influences. Peter was also happy. He wrote to her that for the first time, he felt truly free.

Sadly, after two years, she never again heard from Peter. She later learned from a sailor that Peter had died. After all her struggles and pain, Belle had lost her son forever.

The events of these past few years distressed Belle. Religion, her son, her friends — she believed all these had failed her at some point. In addition, Belle saw how often the rich ignored the poor.

She even felt guilty herself, believing that she took jobs and money away from those who needed them. After all, on one occasion she had pocketed money her employer had given her to hire a poor person to scrub the porch and then got down on her knees to wash it herself. Did she feel herself more deserving than another? And if she were guilty of such selfishness, how could she criticize others?

> *"How can you expect to do good to God unless you first learn to do good to each other?"*
> *Sojourner Truth*

Slowly she came to believe that it was the city that was to blame. "Truly, here the rich rob the poor and the poor rob each other," she said. She had to get out of this environment and find someplace where she could again do God's work.

A new life

It was the summer of 1843. Truth had been working for nine long years at the home of a wealthy white family in New York City. Her discontent with the city had grown, and she wondered where her life would lead next.

Finally, Belle heard God telling her to leave the city and travel east. She was ready. "The Spirit calls me there and I must go," Belle told her employers. She packed up her belongings and set out on foot for a new life on Long Island.

Stopping on the way for a rest, she began to think about this new chapter in her life. She was forty-six years old, her children were grown and gone, and she had few responsibilities except to God. She remembered how in the Bible, God had destroyed the city of Sodom because its people had become so sinful. She thought the people of New York City had become equally sinful. So behind her rose her "second Sodom," and ahead lay her pilgrimage.

Belle felt she had to leave as much of the old life behind her as possible. Just as Moses in the Bible had left slavery in Egypt, Belle too wanted to leave slavery behind forever. "My name was Isabella; but when I left the house of bondage, I left everything behind. I wasn't going to keep anything of Egypt on me, and so I went to the Lord and asked him to give me a new name. And the Lord gave me Sojourner, because I was to travel up and down the land, showing the people their sins, and being a sign unto them."

Later, because her last name had always been that of her master, Sojourner took the name of her new master, God. The Bible spoke of God as Truth. And so on that summer day in 1843, her new life began as Sojourner Truth.

Truth traveled most of the northern United States, an area of over 1,500,000 square miles (3,885,000 sq km). Amazingly, she often went by foot, not knowing where she would be allowed to stop and rest, ignoring the danger of anti-abolitionists along her long journey.

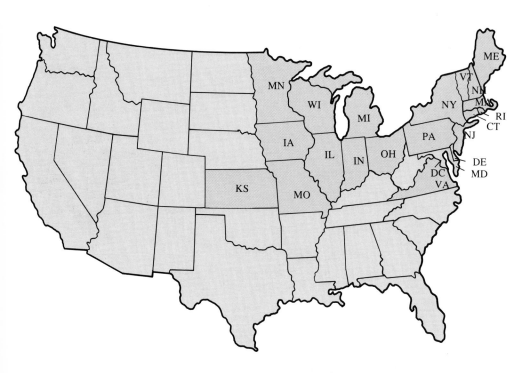

Sojourner speaks her truth

By the time Truth began her journey, she had already left her family behind. Thomas, who was elderly when they had married, had died. Peter too was dead. Her two oldest daughters remained on John Dumont's farm, working for him as free servants. And Sophia, her youngest daughter, had decided to return to Dumont to live with her sisters.

When her daughters learned that their mother had left New York, they became alarmed. They thought they might never see or hear from her again. But Truth dictated letters to her children and maintained her contact with them and with their children until her death. She had struggled too long to keep her family intact and to gain their freedom. She would not let her travels disrupt her devotion.

Truth traveled east for several days, preaching about God and working odd jobs to pay her way. On her travels, she often attended revival meetings, abolitionist meetings, and meetings of temperance groups, groups that urged others to give up alcohol because of the way it had damaged their lives. Sojourner would cook for the people who attended and would sometimes speak. But she wouldn't stay long, saying, "God does not stop to rest, for he is a spirit, and cannot tire." Sojourner expected nearly as much of herself!

Soon Truth's preaching earned her some fame. One newspaper reported that she had "a remarkable gift in prayer and still more remarkable talent for singing." By the time she reached Springfield, Massachusetts, people demanded to hear her speak, and she found several organizations in the state clamoring for her talents.

One, the Northampton Association, a utopian settlement, convinced her to come and visit them. At first it seemed a messy, disorganized place, not the peaceful, well-ordered utopian community she had imagined. But as she stayed and looked about her, she came face to face with an organized public struggle for emancipation. In the past, Truth had always looked upon the fight for freedom as a personal battle. Now she realized that an entire nation needed to rid itself of slavery once and for all.

"Let her tell her story without interrupting her, and give close attention, and you will see she has got the lever of truth, that God helps her to pry where but few can. She cannot read or write, but the law is in her heart."
Church member
in Bristol, Connecticut,
writing to a Hartford church

21

Joining forces

In Truth's earlier contacts with the abolitionists, she had learned of their desire for the emancipation of slaves and equality for blacks. These people and their strong belief had encouraged her to fight for her own freedom. Now, though, she heard how many slaves in the South received brutal beatings, how their families had been torn apart. Suddenly she realized that it wasn't just Peter or her family or the families of the few slaves she knew who were suffering. An entire race was without freedom and, more important, without respect.

This word *respect* would become the cornerstone of Truth's work. Slaves could be made free, women could be given equal rights, people could be given the rights of citizenship, but without respect, nothing mattered. Many women and blacks had long lacked self-respect, had considered themselves second-class, an evaluation promoted by a society that put little value on their thoughts or actions.

Sojourner Truth began to compare her experiences with those of other slaves. She realized that until she had demanded the respect of her white brothers and sisters, she had not really been free. Respect meant that all of society had to regard blacks and women not only as free but as significant and respectable human beings in their own right.

By the force of her words and the example of her behavior, Truth demanded and kept the self-respect she felt every human deserved. Indeed, her own history had taught her the value of an individual's life. She once admitted that she had struck her own children. But when Peter came back from the Gedney farm covered with bruises and gashes, she cried out, realizing that she was "no better than my master" if she beat her own children. After that, she never used violence against them again.

In addition, when Solomon Gedney had heartlessly sold Peter to Fowler, his brother-in-law in Alabama, Sojourner had angrily prayed to God to wreak some vengeance on the family. Not long after Peter was returned to her, Gedney's sister, Eliza Fowler, was murdered by her husband. Fowler had beaten Eliza horribly, killing her.

"But the circumstance which struck us most forcibly was how it was possible for such a number of human beings to exist, packed up and wedged together as tight as they could cram . . . shut out from light or air, and this when the thermometer [stood] . . . at 89°."
Reverend R. Walsh, on inspecting a slave ship in 1807

Opposite: Some Northern black men became powerful leaders and advocates for emancipation. Many women, like Sojourner Truth, were also outspoken and popular, but rarely did advertising mention their contributions.

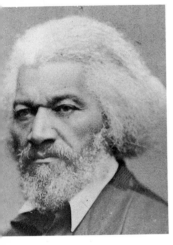

Top: Although William Lloyd Garrison urged that the North secede from the Union because the Constitution permitted slavery, he did not support a violent break. He would not support Abraham Lincoln and the Civil War until Lincoln signed the Emancipation Proclamation.

Bottom: An escaped slave, Frederick Douglass described himself at an abolitionist meeting as "a recent graduate from the institution of slavery with his diploma on his back."

Now Truth regretted making her vengeful prayer. "Oh Lord, I didn't mean all that!" she told God upon hearing news of the murder. The combination of these events — Peter's beatings and Eliza's brutal death — reaffirmed for Truth that violence would never be a solution. Never again did Sojourner Truth advocate violent means.

While at Northampton, Truth heard some of the great abolitionist speakers, including William Lloyd Garrison and Frederick Douglass. Their strength of conviction and their remarkable speaking talent influenced Truth's thinking and style. Instead of just preaching about religion, Truth determined to challenge her listeners to give all people the respect they deserved. And that respect included freedom and equality for everyone.

The power of her truth

Truth had chosen simply to sit and listen at Northampton rather than to speak — until one night. Abolitionists were unpopular with many people. And that night a group of young thugs determined to break up the meeting and attack the participants. As the ruffians stormed into the tent, Truth ran to hide. She was the only black person at the meeting, so she was likely to be a target for the group's anger.

As she hid, she prayed. Suddenly she realized, "Shall I run away and hide from the Devil? Me, a servant of the living God? Have I not faith enough to go out and quell the mob?"

Truth strode out of the tent and up to the top of a nearby hill. With her strong voice, she began to sing. The troublemakers heard her hymns and decided to run at her and beat her. But as they approached, she shouted out, "Why do you come about me with clubs and sticks? I am not doing any harm to any one." Taken aback by her calm reproach and manner, they decided to listen to her instead.

Sojourner climbed on top of a nearby wagon. She sang another hymn, and then she spoke to them and answered their questions. They were spellbound. Her determination and dignity impressed the crowd and commanded their respect. Finally, she asked them to leave in peace, and they agreed.

Her strength that night demonstrated to all about her that Sojourner Truth had forsaken the timidness and subservience of a slave. No one except God would be her master.

Her renown began to grow by word of mouth. In time, Sojourner Truth would become one of the most articulate and forthright advocates in the United States for the rights of blacks and women. That night on the hill, she saw once again that God would give her the strength to combat anger and ignorance. She had been called to her mission: to secure freedom and equality for all people.

"Rachel had the power to move and bear down a whole audience by a few simple words. I never knew but one other human being that had that power, and that other was Sojourner Truth."
Wendell Phillips, abolitionist and social reformer

Antiblack laws and the Dred Scott Decision

Shortly after Truth's visit to Northampton, Congress passed the Fugitive Slave Law in 1850. This law forbade escaped slaves from having a trial by jury, did not allow them to testify in court, and made it a crime for anyone to assist in their escape. Worse, the law was retroactive, which meant every slave who had ever escaped was a criminal! Congress had hoped that the law would calm the Southern plantation owners who were angry that Northern political leaders seemed to ignore the Southerners' need for slave labor and their need for discipline to keep slaves under control on large plantations.

The new law enraged abolitionists, who saw it as a serious step backward in the battle for emancipation. In addition, the Fugitive Slave Act of 1793 was still in force. This act guaranteed that any slave captured would be immediately returned to the owner. Coupled with the recent Fugitive Slave Law, no slave could hope to achieve freedom by escape or through the courts. Both avenues were completely shut off.

One slave who attempted to test these laws became the source of a famous Supreme Court decision. Dred Scott, a Southern slave, had accompanied his master north to free territory, those areas of the United States where slavery was forbidden. He then returned to the South with his master. When his master died, Scott sued for his freedom on the grounds of having lived for some time in a free state. The case went to the Supreme Court.

A photograph of Dred Scott. The Supreme Court's decision on Dred Scott forced political candidates to take a stand on slavery in the free territories. As a presidential candidate, Lincoln assured the South that he wouldn't interfere with slavery where it already existed. But he soon realized that restricting slavery in the free territories meant having to restrict it everywhere.

Harriet Tubman was one of the most successful "conductors" on the Underground Railroad, leading over 300 slaves to freedom. She also worked for the Union army as a spy.

But Scott did not have Truth's legal good fortune. The Court ruled that "any Negro whose ancestors were sold as slaves" was not entitled to the rights of a U.S. citizen. Naturally, this decision effectively smothered any hope of freedom for African-Americans. Most, if not all, blacks in the United States were descended from slaves, so no black could claim the rights of citizenship.

With all these new restrictions on blacks, abolitionists decided on a bold plan. They formed a network of houses, called safe houses, through which slaves could flee to Canada, where laws of the United States did not apply. This network became known as the Underground Railroad.

The power of language

In addition to forming the Underground Railroad, the abolitionists stepped up their resistance to slavery. In Sojourner Truth, they also now had an eloquent former slave who would speak out.

Truth faced many hostile audiences in the years leading up to the Civil War. Many people, even those against slavery, did not want to be taught by a black person. But despite the hostility, Truth knew that if she did not speak out, slavery would be ignored and allowed to continue. "I know what it is to be taken in the barn and tied up and the blood drawed out of your bare back," she would tell her audiences.

During this ten-year period before the Civil War, Truth traveled to twenty-one states and the District of Columbia, covering thousands of miles. Often she had to journey on foot because blacks could not use public transportation. During this time, Truth also adopted the garments she became famous for — a simple, dark dress with a white shawl and a white turban on her head.

Remarkably, many of the white abolitionist audiences did not want to hear the words of "an ignorant, illiterate" black woman. Although they supported emancipation for African-Americans on moral and religious grounds, they didn't consider blacks their equals.

Truth would not be content with people fighting for her freedom if they could not welcome her as their

Truth's carte de visite, *or calling card, shows the traditional gray dress, white shawl, and turban she wore throughout her journeys. She decided that people curious about her gender would want to have a photograph to study and show to friends to get their opinions — was she a woman or a man?*

sister. So she took on the responsibility of convincing these audiences, despite their objections to her speaking. At one rally in 1850 in Syracuse, New York, the white abolitionist George Thompson was the only scheduled speaker, but he yielded the floor to Truth. The crowd jeered, but Sojourner Truth never let that stop her.

"I'll tell you what Thompson is going to say to you. He's going to argue that the poor Negroes ought to be out of slavery and in the heavenly state of freedom. But, children, I'm against slavery because I want to keep the white folks who hold slaves from getting sent to hell!"

Sojourner had spoken the truth. The responsibility belonged to the whites to accept the equality of blacks. The crowd hushed and listened to her speak.

The bite of a flea

Often these abolitionist rallies became a platform for lofty talk about love and peace. Sojourner Truth believed in those values, but she had learned from her experience with The Kingdom that right talk did not always bring right results. At every rally, she stood up

"When I was a slave away down there in New York, and there was some particularly bad work to be done, some colored woman was sure to be called on to do it. And when I heard that man talking away there as he did, almost a whole hour, I said to myself, here's one spot of work sure that's just fit for colored folks to clean up after."
     Sojourner Truth, in response to a man expressing his belief that blacks were nothing more than apes

FREE LECTURE!

SOJOURNER TRUTH,

Who has been a slave in the State of New York, and who has been a Lecturer for the last twenty-three years, whose characteristics have been so vividly portrayed by Mrs. Harriet Beecher Stowe, as the African Sybil, will deliver a lecture upon the present issues of the day,

At   **On**

And will give her experience as a **Slave** mother and religious woman. She comes highly recommended as a public speaker, having the approval of **many** thousands who have heard her earnest appeals, among whom are **Wendell Phillips, Wm. Lloyd Garrison,** and other distinguished men of the nation.

☞ At the close of her discourse she will offer for sale her photograph and a few of her choice songs.

Flyers for Truth's lectures were often distributed only on the day of her lectures. But that didn't hurt attendance. Citizens looked forward to the lectures of visiting celebrities just as many people today look forward to the opening of a new movie. Lectures were inexpensive entertainment and a chance to get out with friends.

and sharply brought the discussion back to action whenever she felt the speakers were getting too abstract or philosophical.

Once, agitated by continued discussions of love and family, Truth rose, weeping visibly.

"We have heard a great deal about love at home in the family. Now children, I was a slave, and my husband and my child were sold from me. . . . Now, husband and child are all gone, and what has become of the affection I had for them? That is the question before the house!"

Ashamed, the audience quickly returned to a discussion of how best to achieve emancipation.

Truth also knew that humor was an effective method for persuading a crowd and quelling her enemies. At an Ohio meeting, a man stood and shouted at Truth, "Old woman, do you think that your talk about slavery does any good? Why, I don't care any more for your talk about slavery than I do for the bite of a flea."

Without hesitation, Sojourner Truth rose and looked the man right in the eye. "Perhaps not, but the Lord willing, I'll keep you scratching."

"Aren't I a woman?"

As Truth traveled the United States in the cause of emancipation, she began to realize how few rights women had. Whenever she wanted a petition signed or sought political support or enlisted religious assistance, she had to ignore women, who made up half of the population. Only men held any power to institute laws or overturn policy.

In 1840, the abolitionist William Lloyd Garrison had gone as a delegate to the World's Anti-Slavery Convention in London, England. Two of his fellow delegates were Lucretia Mott and Elizabeth Cady Stanton, social reformers and feminists from the United States. To his surprise, the convention organizers had refused to seat the two women. Garrison refused to participate until the convention accepted the women, but a motion to have them seated was defeated.

Both Garrison and Stanton returned to the United States determined to fight for both emancipation and women's rights. These issues were both important because laws, physical force, and moral arguments were being used to intimidate and dominate blacks and women.

When Truth met Garrison at the Northampton meeting in 1844, she had dedicated her life to preaching only the gospel. After hearing Garrison speak out against slavery, she was convinced that the

In 1833, Britain banned slavery in the British Empire and halted all shipping of slaves from Africa. Not only did this hurt the supply of slaves for the South, but it also meant that the U.S. government received pressure from Britain to outlaw slavery completely. London became a center of abolitionist activities and conventions.

Women's fashions of the 1840s and 1850s required a tight whalebone corset to create a smooth waistline. Women tied the corsets so tightly that they often could not breathe properly and would then faint. This contributed to the belief that all women were weak and fragile.

emancipation of blacks was the effort God had called her to. But with each speaking engagement, with each moment when she could not exercise any political power, she began to realize with increasing certainty that slavery had many forms. By 1849, Sojourner also spoke out against the subjugation of all women.

At the Woman's Rights Convention of 1851 in Akron, Ohio, Sojourner gave her most eloquent defense of the equality of women. When one man boldly suggested that women were weak and therefore unworthy of equality, Truth could not contain herself.

"That man over there says that women need to be helped into carriages, and lifted over ditches, and to have the best place everywhere. Nobody ever helps me into carriages, or over mud puddles, or gives me any best place, and aren't I a woman? Look at me! Look at my arm! I have plowed, and planted, and gathered into barns, and no man could head me — and aren't I a woman? I could work as much and eat as much as a man (when I could get it), and bear the lash as well — and aren't I a woman?"

If women want rights, why not just take them?

For many years, Sojourner Truth believed that only blacks were not treated with dignity and respect. But the more she thought, observed, and traveled, the more she saw that women too, both black and white, were not given respect. They too were subservient.

Certainly many white men acted kindly toward white women, but Truth knew that kindness could be a trap. While many white men helped their women in and out of carriages and gave them money to buy clothes, they also considered women incapable of political and economic independence. These men would not respect a woman's right to offer an opinion and to exercise the power of the vote. Women had little influence outside the home.

So Truth's lectures began to have three parts: an appeal to religion, an appeal against slavery, and an appeal for women's rights. Many audiences were willing to listen to abolitionist talk but balked at any discussion of women's rights.

Truth knew that women would have to be aggressive in order to combat such prejudice. She knew power had to be taken. But Truth also saw that many women took little action even when men were not present. Rather than demonstrating at voting places, sending delegations to congressmen's offices, or holding public rallies, women would instead gather at women's conventions that only the wealthy could afford to attend. Often these conventions turned into forums for lengthy speeches and few resolutions.

A person of action, Sojourner Truth had little patience with the women's talk. At one point, she rose at a convention to cut the discussion short. "Sisters, I aren't clear what you be after. If women want any rights more than they got, why don't they just take them and not be talking about it?"

She also felt that the women were too concerned with their appearance. The women at these meetings, many of whom were wealthy, often came to these conventions dressed in the latest styles. Many of the hats were quite ornate, prompting Truth to remark: "What kind of reformers be you, with goose-wings on your heads, as if you were going to fly, and dressed in such ridiculous fashion, talking about reform and women rights. 'Pears to me, you had better reform yourselves first."

Truth only meant to encourage them to adopt simple dress like she wore. But some women responded by assuming male attire. These full trousers received the name bloomers from the name of one their advocates, Amelia Jenks Bloomer. But the movement quickly died. Such extreme clothing could not give women equal rights.

The shadow and the substance

Truth continued fighting for the rights of citizenship for African-Americans and women. But her journeys were expensive and all of her speaking engagements had to support her travels. In addition, Truth's home in Northampton, Massachusetts, had a nine-hundred-dollar mortgage on it to be paid in regular installments. Passing the hat rarely gathered the necessary funds to support the tours. In fact, often the funds were stolen right out of the hat as it was passed!

Amelia Jenks Bloomer felt that women couldn't be free and powerful until they got rid of the clutter of corsets and hoops that they wore to be fashionable. Her pants took the place of petticoats and hoops.

Frances Titus traveled with Truth. So did Truth's grandsons, James Caldwell and Sammy Banks. At that time, women rarely traveled alone, for it was neither very safe nor socially acceptable.

Opposite: This photograph shows Truth with papers as if she were reading them. Her supporters sometimes worried that people might not take the ideas of an illiterate woman seriously. So they often played down or tried to hide Truth's inability to read.

Truth needed a more reliable and profitable means of support. In 1845, the former slave Frederick Douglass had published his *Narrative of the Life of Frederick Douglass*. The volume sold well. Even non-abolitionists bought the book out of curiosity.

Olive Gilbert, one of Truth's friends, thought that the narrative of a Northern female slave would be just as popular. She also wanted a book that could serve as a political message for abolitionism.

But Truth despaired about writing a book. Although she was an eloquent speaker, she had never learned to read or to write. She had memorized the Bible by hearing it read often, and she had friends answer her correspondence for her. But a book was different. Truth felt that it would be lying to call the autobiography her book if she did not actually write it. Gilbert had to convince Truth to dictate the book to her and added some abolitionist commentary to the events of Truth's life. The *Narrative of Sojourner Truth* was published in 1850.

Unfortunately the book covered only the years up to Truth's stay at Northampton. So it did not include any material about her own abolitionist and feminist views, only those of other noted abolitionists. After the Civil War, Truth's friend Frances Titus added both her own collection of newspaper clippings about Truth and letters to Truth from fellow abolitionists and feminists. This addition was called *The Book of Life*.

The *Narrative* sold well, but the money often could not reach Truth immediately. She decided that she needed a supplemental form of support. In 1863, a traveling photographer took her picture. She quickly realized the potential of the photograph. Many people had remarked on her striking appearance, so she felt audiences might want to possess a picture of her. She had the portrait printed up on cards with the caption: "I sell the shadow to support the substance." Her picture was merely a shadow of her, but money from these sales would support her. As she had suspected, the portraits sold well.

No matter what her financial state, Truth always believed that a solution would be found. She had a strong group of friends who provided for her. As she put it, "The Lord manages everything."

The nation goes to war

"We are not enemies, but friends. We must not be enemies. Though passion may have strained, it must not break, our bonds of affection."
Abraham Lincoln, referring to the Northern and Southern states

"[I would] . . . welcome the intelligence tomorrow . . . that the slaves had risen in the South, and that the sable arms which had been engaged in beautifying and adorning the South, were engaged in spreading death and devastation."
Frederick Douglass, black abolitionist

"Go quickly and help fill up the first colored regiment from the North. . . . The case is before you. This is our golden opportunity. Let us accept it. . . . Let us win for ourselves the gratitude of our country, and the best blessings of our posterity through all time."
Frederick Douglass, calling on black men to join with the Union forces

For years, the South had felt that the federal government favored the North and meddled far too much in the affairs of the Southern states. One sticking point was the North's insistence that the South should abandon slavery. Naturally, the South felt unfairly singled out. The North did not have plantations requiring large work forces in order to operate effectively. And yet the North gladly accepted the cotton and rice that the South grew.

On the other hand, many citizens, including Southern slave owners, began to believe that slavery was immoral. Still, the South had a principle to uphold. They wanted their sovereignty in affairs that affected only their states.

Finally, tensions between the North and South in the United States could not be resolved through discussion. In 1861, eleven Southern states seceded, or broke away, from the United States.

The Southern states formed their own government, calling themselves the Confederate States of America or the Confederacy, and raised an army, while the North stayed with the administration of President Abraham Lincoln and a government based on the original Constitution. The Northern states still called themselves the United States of America, or the Union. Their main objective was to preserve the federation of all the states, claiming individual states had no right to secede.

The Southern states drafted a new constitution and elected Jefferson Davis as their president. The Northern army kept the color blue for its uniforms while the Southern army was clad in gray. When the Union tried to resupply Fort Sumter, a federal army post in Charleston, South Carolina, the Confederacy opened fire. The Civil War had erupted.

Truth and the abolitionists stepped up their speaking engagements. Now they had to rally participants in this war. If the North lost, then the cause of emancipation would probably also be lost. Both Frederick Douglass and Sojourner Truth encouraged blacks to join with the Union forces. Two of Douglass' sons joined, as did Truth's grandson, James Caldwell.

Truth herself lamented that she was too old to join in the battle physically. If she were younger, she said, "I'd be on hand as the Joan of Arc, to lead the army of the Lord. For now is the day and the hour for the colored man to save this nation."

Although Truth couldn't take up arms, she could bolster the spirits of the men who went to fight. By the time the Civil War began, she had bought a house near Battle Creek, Michigan. She returned to her home to contribute her cooking and speaking talents to the war effort. She adopted the First Michigan Volunteer Infantry (Colored), which was made up of black soldiers, bringing them a feast at Thanksgiving and comforting them with song and encouragement. She even composed lyrics especially for the regiment, to be sung to the tune of "Battle Hymn of the Republic." She wanted these soldiers to have a rallying cry that was uniquely black.

"They will have to pay us wages, the wages of their sin;
They will have to bow their foreheads to their colored kith and kin;
They will have to give us house-room, or the roof will tumble in,
As we go marching on."
A verse of Truth's song for the First Michigan Volunteer Infantry (Colored), sung to the tune of "Battle Hymn of the Republic"

Freeing slaves

At first, the war did not go well for the North. Union President Lincoln and Confederate President Davis had both predicted a swift end to the hostilities. But by the midsummer of 1862, Lincoln knew that the war would last for at least another year. He later admitted, "Things had gone on from bad to worse, until I felt that we had reached the end of our rope on the plan of operations we had been pursuing, that we had about played our last card and must change our tactics or lose the game! I now determined upon the adoption of the emancipation policy."

Lincoln hoped that by freeing the slaves of the South, he would hasten the end of the conflict. On September 22, 1862, he issued his Emancipation Proclamation, freeing all the slaves of the "states . . . in rebellion" on January 1, 1863, and assuring them of safe refuge in the North.

The abolitionists had mixed feelings. Certainly they were pleased that the Southern slaves would now be able to leave the plantations freely without fear of being returned under the Fugitive Slave Law. But what about the slaves of the North? Although most Northern states had individually enacted emancipation acts, some of these acts did not allow for the

Slave owners knew that with the Emancipation Proclamation slaves who made it to free territories would never be returned to them. So some owners decided that the best way to protect their investment was to chase down and kill escaping slaves in the hope of deterring other slaves from attempting escape from the South.

freedom of slaves until their twenty-fifth or twenty-eighth birthday. So while the Southern slaves would be freed immediately, many Northern slaves would have to wait for their emancipation.

The courage to act

Sojourner knew her work on behalf of emancipation was not over yet. But the agitation of war had made the crowds she spoke to even more violent. It was all well and good to support emancipation if it didn't seem to be a reality.

But now Northern whites were faced with the influx of thousands of Southern African-Americans who competed with them for clothing, shelter, and work. Suddenly emancipation didn't seem like such a wise policy.

When she traveled to Indiana, her speeches were disrupted by shouts of "Nigger, nigger!" and "We think the niggers have got enough already." At one rally, the mob was so restless that it would not let her on stage. She finally sneaked past the crowds only after dressing up in a uniform and presenting herself as a member of the home guard, the local militia. When she saw herself so attired, she laughed. "It seems I am going to battle."

It was no surprise that she made an authentic male appearance. Six feet (2 m) tall, with muscular arms and back from the field work she had done as a slave, her face weathered and unadorned with make-up, she did look more male than female.

As the crowds around the country became more and more hostile to Sojourner Truth's message, they looked for ways to discredit her stories. Finally, at one Indiana rally, a man stood up and loudly challenged her gender.

"Your voice is not the voice of a woman, it is the voice of a man, and we believe you are a man."

The crowd then voted on the man's opinion and the ayes won!

Truth rose, angry to be so slandered. Without a sense of false modesty, she silenced the jeers of the crowd by baring her breast. Once again, she recognized that only action, not words, would sufficiently argue her case.

Without the support of abolitionists and freed slaves, many black fighting units would have not had provisions or uniforms. White troops were equipped first.

Equal pay for black soldiers

The blacks of the North and escaped slaves of the South also set out to prove their case with action and joined the Union army. But even as African-Americans began to fight for the Union cause, lawmakers set out to demean their efforts. In July 1863, the War Department ruled that all black troops were to be paid the same as fugitive slaves hired to do menial tasks. These black troops were professional soldiers who often took the most dangerous missions, yet they received the poorest weapons and supplies. Black troops had thought they were fighting alongside their white counterparts when, in fact, they were expected to do more, for less.

Angered, the troops protested, "We have done a soldier's duty. Why can't we have a soldier's pay?" The Fifty-Fourth and Fifty-Fifth Massachusetts Regiments refused to accept *any* pay until Congress eliminated the inequalities. In 1864, Congress finally awarded all the troops equal back pay, but only back to January 1, 1864. It was not until March of 1865 that they received back pay dated from the day they had enlisted.

This picture of Sojourner Truth with Lincoln was actually painted after her death. Truth's daughter, Diana Corbin, posed as Truth, and Lincoln's image was copied from another painting.

Advice to Lincoln

Truth was sixty-four when the Civil War began. She felt herself slowing down and often remarked that she wondered when the work would be done. She had divided her attention on two fronts: abolition and women's rights. Many days she had three or four speaking engagements.

Truth knew that all her speaking out would have little effect if she couldn't persuade the nation's leaders of the justice of her position. Straightforward as always, she decided to go to Washington, D.C., to "advise the president." The war was winding down, and she felt that Lincoln should hear what African-Americans needed.

Lincoln welcomed Sojourner Truth's comments. "I must say, and I am proud to say, that I never was treated by any one with more kindness and cordiality than were shown to me by that great and good man, Abraham Lincoln." The president even took time to autograph her *Book of Life*, a collection of autographs and remarks she collected on her travels: "For Aunty Sojourner Truth, October 29, 1864. A. Lincoln."

"I felt that I was in the presence of a friend, and I now thank God . . . that I always have advocated his cause, and have done it openly and boldly."
Sojourner Truth, on recounting her visit to Abraham Lincoln

Work in Washington, D.C.

In 1864, Truth decided to stop agitating with speeches "way up North" and to come down to Washington, D.C., where she could put her beliefs into action. There, a public welfare organization called the National Freedman's Relief Association asked her to counsel freed slaves in Arlington Heights, Virginia.

Finally, Truth had the legal means to do what she had always wanted to do — help African-Americans achieve economic and moral freedom. Her appointment was a far cry from the "Slaves, horses, and other cattle sold" sign slapped to her chest when she was nine.

After the Emancipation Proclamation freed Southern blacks in 1863, thousands of them had come North. To help them as well as white Civil War refugees, charity organizations and Union agencies had established refugee camps, or freedmen's villages, along Union lines. Many people descended on Washington, D.C., because it was the home of the Great Emancipator, Abraham Lincoln. These were the people Truth worked with.

"With all your opportunities for reading and writing, you don't take hold and do anything. My God, I wonder what you are in the world for!"
Sojourner Truth, to a white audience

Crowded into slums and swamps in the nation's capital, they began to die from disease. White raiders came down to the city and took black children from their families to work in the factories of Northern cities. Once Truth overheard a government agent tell a woman not to make a fuss because her children had been stolen. Immediately, she remembered Mrs. Dumont's words, "Such a fuss over a little nigger," and understood that woman's grief and panic. She helped the woman get the necessary legal assistance to regain her children.

The Freedmen's Bureau

Government officials quickly realized that having so many poor and unhealthy people crowded together would lead to crime and disease. The police superintendent of Washington asked Lincoln to help support this new population. In March 1865, just as the war was ending, the government founded the Freedmen's Bureau to assist the refugees from war. The bureau sought to resettle people in communities where they would find employment and housing.

In 1865, the Freedmen's Bureau appointed Truth to the Freedmen's Hospital of Washington with the words, "give her all facilities and authority." A black woman with authority? Wouldn't Mau-Mau Bett have been proud?

By this time, Sojourner was nearing the age of seventy, but she couldn't slow down, now that all she had fought for was so close. The twenty-six months she spent in Washington gave her a chance to encourage many blacks. She realized that they had to learn to throw off the timidity of their days in slavery. They had to learn how to take control of their lives and futures. She told her grandson, Sammy Banks, who frequently traveled with her, "They have to learn to be free." Every time she spoke to a black man or woman, she used the word *dignity*. Soon her own dignity would once again be tested.

Assassination

On April 9, 1865, Confederate general Robert E. Lee surrendered to Union general Ulysses S. Grant at Appomattox Court House in Virginia. The war was nearly over.

But before the nation could rejoice, John Wilkes Booth assassinated President Lincoln at Ford's Theatre. On April 15, 1865, many admirers mourned the death of this great head of state, who had struggled with the overwhelming problems of economics, states' rights, and human rights.

Truth mourned for the work now left undone. But she also saw that the power to change their status rested with African-Americans themselves. She began to speak out more often, returning North to agitate for the rights of the freed slaves.

Upon Lincoln's death, Vice President Andrew Johnson became president. Unfortunately, Johnson did not share Lincoln's devotion to the cause of equality, and his policies were unpopular. He was a Southerner who wanted to focus on reconstructing the South after the war. He worried more about strengthening the economy of the South than about equal rights. While Northern lawmakers became concerned with the South's economy, Truth became concerned that human rights would be forgotten.

Prejudice continues

Truth realized that the future of blacks in the United States rested with the lawmakers in Washington, D.C. The Emancipation Proclamation had freed the Southern slaves, as of January 1863. In December 1865, the states ratified the Thirteenth Amendment to the Constitution. This amendment abolished all slavery across the United States.

Truth was overjoyed. The long and wearying battle for emancipation was over. She could now focus on ensuring that the federal government really did follow through on the amendment — that it gave freed blacks all the rights of citizenship: the right to vote, to run for office, to own property, and to receive the protection of the law. She wanted to be sure that lawmakers found ways to assist freed slaves.

This would be more difficult than perhaps even she imagined.

In the South, the battle was still for simple freedom. Many Southerners resisted laws passed by the federal government. They believed that they did not have to follow such laws. For years, Southern states had passed their own laws, the Black Codes. These controlled Southern blacks. They restricted travel, kept blacks from leaving their plantations, even regulated when they could shop.

This is a drawing of a freedmen's village. The area looked spacious, but in reality the homes were closely packed shacks. Some people were unprepared for the harshness of the Virginia winters. They expected the temperate climate of the Southern locales they had fled.

"Sojourner Truth has good ideas about the industry and virtue of the colored people. I commend her energetic and faithful efforts . . . so far as she can aid . . . in promoting order, cleanliness, industry, and virtue among the patients."

John Eaton, Jr., on appointing Sojourner to the Freedmen's Bureau

In order to maintain these codes, white citizens created private enforcement groups, called vigilante groups. They would ride around looking for blacks who broke these codes — or who were just in the wrong place at the wrong time. Often the retaliation was swift and without a trial. Blacks were lynched, their homes burned, their children stolen.

In 1865, out of these vigilante groups, rose one that gained widespread acceptance — the Ku Klux Klan. In its early years, Klan members intimidated African-Americans and ruthlessly administered their own "justice" without benefit of the U.S. legal system. The hatred that the Ku Klux Klan preached affected the way many whites regarded blacks and reinforced the prejudice Truth fought to eliminate.

The Jim Crow car

The Black Codes had long controlled many areas of black life. Then, after the Civil War had ended, Jim Crow laws appeared. According to Jim Crow laws, blacks and whites had to be separated, or segregated, in transportation, work, and entertainment.

JIM CROW LAW.

PHELD BY THE UNITED STATES SUPREME COURT.

tatute Within the Competency of the Louisiana Legislature and Railroads—Must Furnish Separate Cars for Whites and Blacks.

Many legislators tried to abolish Jim Crow laws. They argued that having "separate but equal" facilities for blacks and whites made as much sense as having separate facilities for Protestants and Catholics or for short and tall people.

Blacks and whites drank out of separate drinking fountains, used separate bathrooms, sat in different parts of the theater, rode in different parts of the train, and went to different schools. These separate facilities were supposed to be equally nice but, in fact, they were not. Those areas set aside for African-Americans were never as nice as those for whites. Sojourner Truth would not accept this. In Washington, she had been riding in a separate street-car, set aside just for African-Americans.

Here she was, in the Freedmen's Hospital, assuming a great deal of responsibility. She was not going to have the authority to run a hospital and then have no authority to choose the streetcar she rode home in! She complained to the president of the street railroad in Washington, who promptly ordered the Jim Crow car taken off.

Unfortunately, this angered many conductors. Up until then, they had tolerated the black passengers as long as they did not not mix with the white. Laws can demand a change of behavior, but not a change of heart. So to avoid mixing white people and black

42

people, the conductors simply refused to stop for blacks. Most blacks accepted this show of racism, but not Truth.

One summer day, in 1867, after a long shift at the hospital, she wanted to get home to rest, but the streetcar did not stop. She took flight and chased it down until the conductor stopped and she boarded. On another occasion, a conductor tried to toss her off the car. When pushing her off, he wrenched her arm so badly that she sued him for damages. She won. Truth knew action was the only solution. She might not change their hearts, but she could get them to obey the law. And she would demand that she be treated with respect.

But whose rights?

The Thirteenth Amendment had freed the slaves but did not make them citizens. Nor did the Constitution assure women of these same rights of citizenship. Just as Garrison and Stanton had argued, the issues of blacks and women were closely aligned.

But women's rights advocates, including Truth, put great faith in the eventual citizenship of African-Americans. They believed that once the lawmakers in Washington began to discuss the issue of black citizenship, the government would have no choice but to grant women equal rights. At one rally, Truth

"There is a great stir about colored men getting their rights, but not a word about the colored women; and if colored men get their rights, and not colored women theirs, you see the colored men will be masters over the women, and it will be just as bad as it was before. So I am for keeping the thing going while things are stirring; because if we wait till it is still, it will take a great while to get it going again."
Sojourner Truth

Giving blacks equal rights didn't ensure respect for them. Ridicule of blacks was encouraged as a way to satirize political issues. Portraying blacks in "Darktown" as incompetent may have seemed funny to some, but it also reinforced prejudice against blacks as an "inferior" class.

"If the first woman God ever made was strong enough to turn the world upside down, all alone, these together ought to be able to turn it back and get it right side up again, and now they are asking to do it, the men better let them."
Sojourner Truth,
to the Woman's Rights
Convention of 1854

"When I ran away from slavery, it was for myself; when I advocated emancipation, it was for my people; but when I stood up for the rights of woman, self was out of the question, and I found a little nobility in the act."
Frederick Douglass, former
slave, abolitionist, and
women's rights advocate

"But we'll have our rights; see if we don't; and you can't stop us from them; see if you can. You may hiss as much as you like, but it is coming. Women don't get half as much rights as they ought to; we want more, and we will have it."
Sojourner Truth,
to the Woman's Rights
Convention of 1853

argued that giving black men — but not black women — citizenship would mean that black women would continue to be slaves under new masters. How could they give only black *men* rights?

The white women advocates reasoned, with prejudice, that they certainly had more right to citizenship than did black men. So once the government realized the necessity of granting full citizenship to black men, they would have to grant it to all women as well. They argued that, during the war, women active in the women's rights movement had set aside their political agitation to focus their attention on the war effort. If they were willing to protect these rights, then shouldn't they be allowed them?

Shortly after President Lincoln's death, the Congress approved the Fourteenth Amendment, which the states ratified in 1868. This amendment made laws against blacks unconstitutional (although within individual states, Jim Crow laws lasted for years). But when the wording of the Fourteenth Amendment was made public, the women's rights advocates were shocked. This amendment not only excluded women indirectly, but also directly. It was the only place in the entire U.S. Constitution where legislators carefully specified the term *male*! There was no mistaking what the lawmakers intended — women had no right to citizenship.

Even more appalling to Truth was the opening language of the amendment: "All persons born or naturalized in the United States . . . are citizens." That meant that many blacks were denied citizenship because they were born in Africa. The government had not come through as she had hoped.

"We do as much, we eat as much, we want as much!"

Then, in 1870, the states ratified the Fifteenth Amendment, guaranteeing the right to vote without respect to race, color, or previous servitude. But not to sex! It was time to begin speaking out again.

Truth was now seventy-three years old. In the late 1800s, it was an achievement just to be alive at seventy-three. She suffered from leg ulcers as Mau-Mau Bett, her mother, had, and in 1863, she had

44

nearly died from an infection. But Truth knew she couldn't rest and couldn't complain about her age. Women had been neglected, and they needed strong voices raised in their defense.

While Truth had once believed that only black women would face continued subjugation, she now accepted that all women suffered from oppression. Despite this, she felt that black women were at more of a disadvantage than white women. White women could enjoy some of the rights of citizenship through their marriage to white men, who had fuller economic and political opportunities than black men. Because African-Americans had been sold so frequently, family ties, even marital ties, were often lost. Black women had no relatives or husbands they could depend on, and many black women had to work to support themselves and their families. But the wages they earned never compared to the men's, even to black men's wages. So Truth often spoke up specifically in their defense.

"I have done a great deal of work; as much as a man, but did not get so much pay. I used to work in the field and bind grain, keeping up with the cradler but men doing no more, got twice as much pay. . . . We do as much, we eat as much, we want as much."

The press attempted to justify the subjugation of women and African-Americans. "How did the

Ratifying the Fourteenth and Fifteenth Amendments was a major triumph for abolitionists. But blacks had an entire history of prejudice still to fight. The rights of citizenship were of little use to blacks who were considered inferior, fit for only the most menial jobs. These blacks had their days filled just trying to survive.

"Well, children, where there is so much racket there must be something out of kilter. I think that 'twixt the niggers of the South and the women at the North all talking about rights, the white men will be in a fix pretty soon."
Sojourner Truth

45

woman first become subject to man, as she now is all over the world? By her nature, her sex, just as the Negro is and always will be to the end of time inferior to the white race and, therefore, doomed to subjection; but she is happier than she would be in any other condition, just because it is the law of her nature." Law of her nature? Truth didn't possess a nature that welcomed subjugation, and she didn't expect that many other blacks or women did either.

Some men also suggested that women did not have enough intellect to be citizens with the right to vote. Truth quickly put them in their place. "What's [intellect] got to do with women's rights or niggers' rights? If my cup won't hold but a pint and yours a quart, wouldn't you be mean not to let me have my little half-measure full?"

Truth knew that the issue might seem to be a different one, women's rights, but the issue was really still slavery. Speaking to a group of men, she chided them, "You have been having our rights so long, that you think, like a slave-holder, that you own us. I know that it is hard for one who had held the reins for so long to give up; it cuts like a knife. It will feel all the better when it closes up again."

Help to break the chain

Despite efforts of women all over the United States, legislators refused to consider the issue of women's rights. Many women began to accept Truth's message that action should always accompany words. Women began to appear at polling booths to try to register to vote and, failing that, to attempt to vote anyway.

Occasionally they succeeded. In 1871, Nannette B. Gardner wrote to Sojourner from Detroit: "I record the fact that I succeeded in registering my name in the First Precinct of the Ninth Ward, and on Tuesday, the 4th of April, cast the first vote for a state officer deposited in an American ballot-box by a woman."

Still the triumphs were few and made little impression. Truth herself attempted to vote on several occasions and didn't intend to stop trying. Even the public knew; as one Battle Creek reporter wrote, "It is Sojourner's determination to continue the assertion of her rights, until she gains them."

"Did Jesus ever say anything against women? Not a word. But he did speak awful hard things against the men. You know what they were. And he knew them to be true. But he didn't say nothing against the women."

Sojourner Truth

"Now I hear talking about the Constitution and the rights of man. I come up and I take hold of this Constitution. It looks mighty big, and I feel for my rights, but there aren't any there. Then I says, God, what ails this Constitution? He says to me, 'Sojourner, there is a little weevil in it.'"

Sojourner Truth

The women focused on the right to vote because it gave them the power to get other rights. If they could unite half the population, they could accomplish so much. They could elect men and women sympathetic to women's issues. They could enact laws ensuring equal pay. They could strike down laws giving men favored economic and political status. This, of course, is exactly what many male voters feared.

Truth believed that winning equal rights for all humans was an edict from God. She knew that as long as God's work was unfinished, she must fight. Many of the women she spoke with asked why she continued. "I suppose I am kept here because something remains for me to do. I suppose I am yet to help to break the chain." She fought for women's rights up to her death but never lived to see women achieve the right to vote. She also never surrendered.

Trapped in the slums

Even as she was speaking out for women's right to vote, Truth could not forget the poverty and congested living conditions of the blacks in the Northern cities. Most had been field slaves who knew about farming but not about life in crowded city slums. She felt the government owed these former slaves something. While traveling around Washington, D.C., she was overwhelmed by the gleaming monuments and spoke out, "We helped to pay this cost!"

Truth lectured one audience: "We have been a source of wealth to this republic. Our labor supplied the country with cotton, until villages and cities dotted the . . . North. . . . We toiled . . . urged on by the merciless driver's lash." Now these same slaves were trapped in the filthy slums of the cities they helped to build, uncompensated for all their contributions.

Meanwhile, the West was opening up. Thousands of acres of land had been given free to the railroads to support the expansion. Truth knew that the railroads could not possibly use all that land, so she proposed that the western lands be given to the freed slaves. So in 1870, for the second time, she requested an audience with a U.S. president. This time it was Ulysses S. Grant, the former general of the Union army. As a reporter said about the meeting, "Grant

"You ask me what to do for them? Do you want a poor old creature who doesn't know how to read to tell educated people what to do? I give you the hint, and you ought to know what to do."
Sojourner Truth, at a rally in favor of compensation for emancipated slaves

"Our nerves and sinews, our tears and blood, have been sacrificed on the altar of this nation's avarice. Our unpaid labor has been a stepping-stone to its financial success. Some of its dividends must surely be ours."
Sojourner Truth, to the U.S. Congress in hopes of getting compensation for the emancipated slaves

"[President Grant asked] 'How old do you call yourself now?' I had felt very much annoyed by peoples calling to me in the street and asking that question. . . . Dr. Howland . . . advised me to charge five dollars for answering that question."
Sojourner Truth, 1870

was reticent yet kindly," not nearly as receptive as Lincoln had been. In April of 1870, Truth also went to a joint session of Congress to propose her plan. One congressman noted that Congress would do nothing unless the people requested it.

So she asked that he help her draw up a petition: "Whereas . . . we believe that the freed colored people in and about Washington, dependent upon government for support, would be greatly benefited and might become useful citizens by being placed in a position to support themselves: We . . . request your honorable body to set apart for them a portion of public land in the West."

Renewed hatred

While speaking out for women's rights, Truth circulated her petition. She even made a special trip to Kansas to get support from settlers there.

On this trip, Truth felt the sting of personal attack. She had met hatred before but never had anyone spoken out directly against her. Now the press saw her petition as a threat to the white settlers in the new western territories. In Springfield, New Jersey, one reporter wrote: "We do most decidedly dislike the complexion and everything else appertaining to Mrs. Truth. . . . She is a crazy, ignorant, repelling negress." The attacks only strengthened her efforts.

While many papers attacked her personally, other papers willingly took up the cause of land for blacks. One Rochester, New York, paper wrote: "Her subject is the condition of the freed colored people dependent on the government. . . . Let Rochester give her a cordial reception." Still, newspapers were reluctant to take a stand, although they kept the issue alive by reporting Truth's remarks. "Let the freedmen be emptied out in the West; give them land; . . . teach them to read, and then they will be somebody." Despite attacks and the reluctance of the press, Truth resolved to get black people land of their own, so they would no longer be, as she called them, "trash" in the streets of Washington.

All these efforts took a toll on the elderly woman. Back in 1863, she had become very ill and many thought she would not survive. Even Harriet Beecher

Abraham Lincoln called Harriet Beecher Stowe the "little lady who wrote the book that made this great war." Uncle Tom's Cabin *forced people to seriously consider the treatment of slaves through sympathetic slave characters like Topsy and Little Eva, as well as through the classic villain, Simon Legree.*

Stowe, author of *Uncle Tom's Cabin*, wrote an article about her saying, "But though Sojourner Truth has passed away from us as a wave of the sea, her memory still lives."

But Truth was not to be so quickly taken from her tasks. She tried to secure land for the slaves and the right to vote for women. She once told Frederick Douglass, "I never determined to do anything and failed." And so she had continued to journey.

"Her whole air had at times a gloomy sort of drollery which impressed one strangely."
Harriet Beecher Stowe, on meeting Sojourner Truth

Tragedy and declining health

But by 1880, Sojourner had reached her limits of physical exertion. The struggle to speak out on so many issues of importance had taken away her strength to combat illness. For ten long years she had traveled to twenty-one states and the District of Columbia, often lecturing at a different town each day. Many of these journeys had been by foot. Her leg ulcers continued to fester. In 1875, she had lost her favorite grandson, Elizabeth's son Sammy Banks, who had also been her traveling companion since he was five. He was only twenty-five years old at his death. The depression she felt made her sleepless, further weakening her.

Sojourner had also weakened her health through smoking. Once a follower criticized her for this habit because it left her breath so foul, saying: "No unclean thing can enter the kingdom of Heaven." Always quick to defend herself, Truth replied that when she went to heaven, "I expect to leave my breath behind." Nevertheless, her failing health soon made smoking impossible. Amy Post reported to the *National Anti-Slavery Standard* that now Truth "has laid it all aside, has not smoked once, in three months."

"The Lord has put new flesh on to old bones."
Sojourner Truth, when her leg ulcer healed for a time

Despite her illness, she did manage to travel to the Philadelphia Centennial Exposition to celebrate the one-hundredth birthday of the United States. Here she lectured for the granting of land parcels to former slaves and the continued growth of the nation through government by men and women united. But the effort grew increasingly wearying.

"Won't that be glorious!"

Until her death, she returned more and more often to her home in Battle Creek, Michigan. Her neighbors were delighted to have the famous Sojourner Truth back home and were eager to help out. Her physician was Dr. John Kellogg of the Kellogg cereal family. He cared for her to the best of his ability, but she was a stubborn patient. As soon as she began to feel better, she would leave for another speaking tour.

"Well, doctor, I thought those salves and other medicines you gave me were too mild for anyone as tough as I am, so I went to the horse doctor and he gave me something that was real strong!"
Sojourner Truth

By 1883, her leg ulcers had become too serious to heal. Kellogg tried several different salves, but he told her friends not to expect recovery. His active patient took it upon herself to test out other salves when his prescriptions didn't work, even using a salve meant for horses! For the first time, her policy of action backfired. The horse salve only made her ulcers worse. She suffered fevers that made her unconscious. Friends began to gather in Battle Creek anticipating her death.

Even so, Truth would not quit fighting. Between fevers she still dictated letters and encouraged her followers to fight for western lands. It grieved her that much of what she had fought for was still unfinished.

50

Forty years after her death, the citizens of Battle Creek, Michigan, erected a memorial to Sojourner Truth's family, who is also buried at this site. Once a year the local historical society stages a pageant to celebrate Truth's contributions to the struggle for blacks' and women's rights.

She continued to express her faith in God. Death for her was a beginning. So although she was leaving behind unfinished work, she knew that God would provide her with a new task in heaven. In one interview, she compared death to stepping out of one room into another, stepping out into the light. "Oh, won't that be glorious!" she cried. Even on her deathbed she consoled her friends and children, "I'm not going to die, honey; I'm going home like a shooting star." On November 26, 1883, Truth died.

Adulation

Much of the nation's disfavor with this "uppity" black woman melted away at the news of her death. Many people had disagreed with her politics, but they respected her determination. Papers across the United States recognized how tirelessly she had fought for her beliefs. One Battle Creek paper wrote, "This country has lost one of its most remarkable personages." Frederick Douglass, on losing one of his strongest allies, wrote, "She was a woman venerable for age, distinguished for insight into human nature, remarkable for independence and courageous self-assertion." More than one thousand people attended her funeral.

In 1904, the Daughters of the American Revolution, at the time a white women's organization, began a collection to have her grave properly marked, a fitting tribute to Sojourner's attempt to unite people of all colors. In 1916, a marble headstone was placed on the site, and in 1946, a more permanent granite tombstone replaced it.

The citizens of Battle Creek worked to maintain the memory of Truth and her ideas. Besides the grave markers, they established a museum to house and celebrate the record of her accomplishments. They also encouraged the Detroit Historical Museum to hang a portrait of Truth.

Despite the efforts of the citizens of Battle Creek, Truth remains unknown to many people in the world. Although her work encompassed so many important causes, her name has been overshadowed by such contemporaries as Frederick Douglass and Susan B. Anthony. Perhaps because she was illiterate and could leave no written legacy except her *Narrative*, she has not maintained a place in historic memory. But despite this lack of recognition, the work she undertook provided the basis for further advancement of women and African-Americans. Her words have been remembered, her lessons followed, by other important world figures.

The legal legacy of Sojourner Truth

Truth was part of a visionary movement of her time, indeed, strode to the forefront of a civil rights movement that continues over one hundred years after her death. Sojourner did not live to win all the battles she fought. But she did know that her work would be continued by others equally committed to the causes. While, sadly, many of the struggles continue, many have ended with victory. For example, women's right to vote was secured in 1920 when the states ratified the Nineteenth Amendment.

In 1964 the Twenty-fourth Amendment, known as the Poll Tax Amendment, was ratified. Although black men had been given the vote in 1870 and women in 1920, some Southern states tried to keep people from voting by enacting poll taxes that had to be paid to election officials before citizens could vote.

Opposite: Guided by the Bible, the successes of Mahatma Gandhi, and his readings on the history of emancipation, the Reverend Martin Luther King, Jr., encouraged African-Americans to press for their equal rights through nonviolent protest. Truth's own fiery speeches and advice to women and blacks served to inspire King's involvement and dedication to the civil rights movement.

This tax effectively kept most blacks and poor whites from being able to vote. They simply could not afford it. Voting districts with such a tax claimed that they were not discriminating because all voters had to pay. But in reality, most whites could afford the cost, thus ensuring a white majority even in predominantly black voting districts. The Poll Tax Amendment outlawed these poll taxes as a form of discrimination.

In the years after the Poll Tax Amendment, many more laws were passed that further guaranteed the rights of citizenship to minorities. In 1964 and 1968, two Civil Rights Acts were passed. Together, these acts prohibited discrimination in employment, federally financed housing, and public accommodations, such as hotels, restaurants, and theaters, for reasons of color, race, religion, gender, or national origin. In 1965, the Voting Rights Act passed, banning the use of literacy or voter-qualification tests that were sometimes used to keep African-Americans from registering to vote.

In 1972, one hundred years after Truth had spoken out so strongly in favor of equality, Congress passed the Equal Rights Amendment. It would have assured all citizens equal rights under the law regardless of sex. But not enough states voted to ratify this amendment, and in 1982, three states short of final passage, it failed to become part of the Constitution.

Organized power

The banner that Truth's struggle for human rights helped to raise was carried after her death not only by individuals but by organizations. These groups owe their power to the early abolitionist and women's rights movements of the 1800s.

One of these, the National Association for the Advancement of Colored People (NAACP) was formed in 1909, its primary purpose to eradicate racism and to abolish lynching. Often, especially when a black man was accused of a crime, local groups of white men took the law into their own hands and executed the accused by hanging. The NAACP wanted local authorities to ensure that blacks got their right to trial as guaranteed in the Constitution. By 1950, lynchings were not as common.

W.E.B. DUBOIS CLUB
HOUGH PROJECT

JOBS
PEACE
FREEDOM

JOBS
PEACE
FREEDOM

"Fellow Negroes, is it not time to be men? Is it not time to strike back when we are struck? Is it not high time to hold up our heads and clench our teeth and swear by the Eternal God we will not be slaves and that no aider, abettor, and teacher of slavery in any shape or guise can longer lead us?"
W.E.B. DuBois, The Crises, 1913 (from Freedomways, 1st quarter, 1965.)

JOIN
NOW

FREEDOM
NOW

1844 E. 81ST • PHONE: 791-5179

W. E. B. Du Bois earned a Ph.D. from Harvard University and taught economics and history at Atlanta University. But with all his education, he could not even drink from the same water fountain as whites or sit in the same section of the courthouse. Along with others, he formed an organization, which was called the National Association for the Advancement of Colored People. It would give African-Americans the political power to fight such injustices.

But segregation persisted, supported both by Jim Crow laws and by local customs. Many aspects of life, such as housing, schooling, employment, public services, and even health care, were separated along racial lines. When the races were segregated, blacks often ended up with the worst housing, the worst schools, and the worst jobs.

Laws also prevented blacks from using the same facilities as whites, facilities such as restaurants, hotels, drinking fountains, and bathrooms. Even Truth had had the right to use all the "white" facilities once she gained her freedom! While the NAACP protested discriminatory laws through the courts, African-Americans and their supporters also formed organizations such as the National Urban League and the Southern Christian Leadership Conference, using boycotts, strikes, legal battles, and peaceful demonstrations to change both laws and customs.

Encouraged by the successes of the black civil rights movement, women in the United States began to organize to gain their rights too. The National Organization for Women (NOW) formed in 1966 to support full equality for women. NOW has achieved a number of successes in women's rights. One of its most important issues — equal pay for equal work —

55

Over one hundred years after the first women's rights convention, women continue to organize to fight for women's issues. The women in this photograph raise their hands in a salute to the Equal Rights Amendment at the 1977 national convention of the National Organization for Women (NOW).

was a cause Sojourner advocated on her travels. In recognition of Truth's work, several chapters of NOW are named after her.

Truth was also at the forefront of a battle that has only recently resumed — the fight against domestic violence. She felt that beatings not only hurt people physically but also took away their dignity. Whenever she saw people using brutality to gain their way, she stepped in to try to stop them. Today many programs for abused women operate under the name of Sojourner Truth in recognition of her work.

Fellow champions of equality

Principles of equality, freedom, and nonviolence continued to have an impact, not only in the United States but throughout the world, through the efforts of two modern leaders, Martin Luther King, Jr., and Mahatma Gandhi.

Because Sojourner could not write, her words could not carry easily to other nations. It was only through word of mouth, newspapers, and the books that others wrote for her that her ideas were spread. Other abolitionists did write, and their work reached England. There these writings came to the attention of a law student from India, Mohandas Gandhi. When

Gandhi returned to his home in South Africa, he also pursued the teachings of Quakers he met there, especially their doctrine of nonviolence, the same doctrine Truth supported.

Having seen so much brutality, Truth had decided she could no longer use force against others. Gandhi promoted nonviolence on a larger scale. He added elements of his Hindu religion to the principles he learned from reading the ideas of the abolitionists and Quakers. He saw nonviolent protest as an organized way to secure human rights. It was a way for Indians to demand freedom from their British rulers. He organized protests that dramatically demonstrated the brutal trampling of human rights in India. The more violently the British reacted to these peaceful demonstrations, the more the world admired the Indians.

Like Truth, Gandhi argued that it was impossible for anyone to be free as long as some people lived without equality. But he was ahead of his time. He also realized that winning freedom for India was pointless if women there did not have the full rights of citizenship. So while championing the rights of Indians, he asked that the new Indian constitution guarantee equal rights for women and encouraged the Indians to abolish the Hindu caste system.

"I have a dream that one day this nation will rise up and live out the true meaning of its creed: 'We hold these truths to be self-evident: that all men are created equal.' I have a dream that one day on the red hills of Georgia the sons of former slaves and the sons of former slave-owners will be able to sit down together at the table of brotherhood. . . . I have a dream that my four little children will one day live in a nation where they will not be judged by the color of their skin, but by the content of their character."

Martin Luther King, Jr., in his famous 1963 speech

Opposite: Truth enjoyed passing herself off as older than she really was. She thought that her "old age" earned her some attention and respect for her issues. Since Sojourner looked so old and leathery, many people believed her to be well over one hundred years old, although she was actually about eighty-six when she died.

"When we follow her from one field of labor to another, her time being divided between teaching, preaching, nursing, watching, and praying, ever ready to counsel, comfort, and assist, we feel that, for one who is nobody but a woman, an unlettered woman, a black woman, and an old woman, a woman born and bred a slave, nothing short of the Divine incarnated in the human, could have wrought out such grand results."
Frances Titus, Sojourner Truth's friend and traveling companion

In the mid-twentieth century, in the United States, an African-American was carrying on the spirit of Truth and Gandhi. Martin Luther King, Jr., an admirer of Gandhi and his ideas, led the black civil rights struggle during the 1950s and 1960s. This movement was trying to ensure that the government carried through on the promise of equal rights it had made to blacks nearly a century before. One civil rights group, the Student Nonviolent Coordinating Committee (SNCC), based its philosophy on the ideas of abolitionists such as Garrison, Phillips, Douglass, and Truth. King advised SNCC and encouraged members to follow the principles of nonviolence. One SNCC tactic was to enter a place of business where blacks were excluded and sit down, refusing to move until they were either served or forcibly removed. These "sit-ins" publicized injustices done to blacks.

"I have done the best I could"

Few memorials stand to Sojourner, and few people know of her achievements. Ironically, in Detroit, one public housing building named after her was the site of race riots in 1942. Three black families trying to move in were met by a mob of twelve hundred whites who attacked them with knives, bottles, and guns. It took two months and the protection of eight hundred state troopers before the families could stay.

When she left Dumont's farm in 1826, Sojourner knew that her journey would not be easy. But it would be a journey she controlled. In every crisis of her life, Truth took action and demanded that justice be done.

Sojourner spent her life acting like a flea, biting at the consciences of the people of the United States and making them scratch. Now more and more people are learning about her struggle and her strength. Her actions and her words linger in the civil rights and women's rights movements today.

Sojourner Truth knew that she would not live to see all her work accomplished. But she believed that because it was right, it would eventually be done. She lived up to her name, traveling the road to freedom and respect, telling people the truth about injustice. As she was dying, she told her friends, "I have done the best I could. I have told the whole truth."

For More Information . . .

Organizations

Write to the organizations listed below if you would like more information about Sojourner Truth and about the civil and women's rights movements. Some may have newsletters or magazines that will provide you with information. Also check your phone book; many cities have local chapters of these groups that you may call. When you write to them, explain exactly what you would like to know, and include your name, address, and age.

The King Center
449 Auburn Avenue NE
Atlanta, GA 30312

Communiqu'Elles
3585 St.-Urbain
Montreal, Quebec
Canada H2X 2N6

National Urban League, Inc.
500 East 62nd Street
New York, NY 10021

National Action Committee on the
    Status of Women
344 Bloor Street West, Suite 505
Toronto, Ontario
Canada M5S 3A7

Detroit Public Library
5201 Woodward Avenue
Detroit, MI 48202

Kimball House Museum
196 Capital Avenue NE
Battle Creek, MI 49017

National Organization for Women (NOW)
1000 16th Street NW, Suite 700
Washington, DC 20036

National Association for the Advancement
    of Colored People (NAACP)
4805 Mount Hope Drive
Baltimore, MD 21215

Congress of Black Women
    of Canada
756 Offington Avenue
Toronto, Ontario
Canada N6G 3T9

Ontario Black History Society
Ontario Heritage Center
10 Adelaide Street East, Suite 202
Toronto, Ontario
Canada M5C 1J3

Batterers Anonymous Beyond
    Abuse Program
P.O. Box 08110
Milwaukee, WI 53208

Books

The following books will help you learn more about Sojourner Truth and slavery and about the civil rights and women's rights movements. Check your local library or bookstore to see if they have them or can order them for you.

About Sojourner Truth —

Journey Toward Freedom: The Story of Sojourner Truth. Bernard
    (Grosset & Dunlap)
Sojourner Truth. Krass (Chelsea House)

Sojourner Truth, A Self-Made Woman. Ortiz (J. B. Lippincott Junior)
Sojourner Truth: Slave, Abolitionist, Fighter for Women's Rights. Lindstrom
   (Julian Messner)
Sojourner Truth and the Struggle for Freedom. Claflin (Barron's Educational Series)
Walking the Road to Freedom: A Story about Sojourner Truth. Ferris
   (Carolrhoda Books)

About Slavery and Emancipation —

Captive Bodies, Free Spirits: The Story of Southern Slavery. Evitts (Julian Messner)
Escape. Bonin (Loft, Barnell)
Frederick Douglass: Freedom Fighter. Patterson (Garrard)
Harriet and the Runaway Book: The Story of Harriet Beecher Stowe and Uncle Tom's
   Cabin. Johnston (Harper & Row Junior Books)
Harriet Tubman: Guide to Freedom. Epstein and Epstein (Garrard)
I Speak for My Slave Sister: The Life of Abby Kelly Foster. Bacon (Crowell
   Junior Books)
The Long Bondage: 1441-1815. McCague (Garrard)
The Slave Dancer. Fox (Bradbury)
To Be a Slave. Lester (Dial Books for Young Readers)
The Truth about the Man Behind the Book That Sparked the War Between the States.
   Cavanah (Westminster Press)
Uncle Tom's Cabin. Stowe (Airmont)
Young Frederick Douglass: Fight for Freedom. Santrey (Troll Associates)

About Civil and Women's Rights —

The Civil Rights Movement in America from 1865 to the Present. Frederick and
   McKissock (Childrens Press)
Elizabeth Cady Stanton. Kendall (Highland Publishing Group)
Every Kid's Guide to Understanding Human Rights. Berry (Childrens Press)
Human Rights. Bradley (Franklin Watts)
The Human Rights Book. Meltzer (Farrar, Straus & Giroux)
Mahatma Gandhi. Nicholson (Gareth Stevens)
Martin Luther King, Jr. Schloredt (Gareth Stevens)
The Story of Susan B. Anthony. Clinton (Childrens Press)
Susan B. Anthony: Champion of Women's Rights. Monsell (Macmillan)
Susan B. Anthony: Pioneer in Woman's Rights. Peterson (Garrard)
Up with Hope: A Biography of Jesse Jackson. Chaplike (Dillon Press)
Women for Human Rights. Conta (Raintree)
Women with a Cause. Wayne (Garrard)
You Can't Do That To Me! Famous Fights for Human Rights. Archer (Macmillan)

Glossary

abolitionism
   A movement with religious roots that opposed slavery on moral grounds and worked
   to end it. Abolitionism began in Britain and France during the late eighteenth century
   and spread to the United States a few years later, gaining support during the

American Revolution. Before the Civil War, abolitionists also worked to improve conditions for Northern blacks by protesting segregation and establishing schools and libraries. They also protected escaped slaves from the South, in particular by forming the Underground Railroad. Abolitionism takes its name from the word *abolish*, which means "to do away with" or "to end."

African-American

A term most recently used to refer to people known in North America as *blacks*. Over the centuries, the language referring to the people now known as *blacks* or *African-Americans* has changed. Slaves brought to the Americas in the seventeenth and eighteenth century were simply called *Africans* by slave traders and owners. But among themselves, the Africans referred to themselves as *blacks*. During the eighteenth century, the term *Negro* came into use, from the Spanish and Portuguese word *negro*.

Although no one knows how the term *nigger* came into use, it may have come from slurring the word *Negro*. While black people have used *nigger* as an intimate term, it is also an insult, particularly when uttered by nonblacks. It is commonly acknowledged to be the most insulting term for blacks in English-speaking North America. During the eighteenth and nineteenth centuries, as whites and blacks gave birth to children with varying tints of brown in their skin, the term *colored* became common. During the civil rights movements of the 1960s, the term *black* again became popularly accepted, and today people use both *African-American* and *black*.

aunty

A charitable or helpful woman. This term was often used to refer respectfully to elderly black women.

chattel

A movable item of personal property, like furniture, an automobile, or an animal. Slaves were also considered chattels.

Douglass, Frederick (1817-1895)

An escaped slave who campaigned against slavery. A fiery orator, Douglass risked possible recapture and slavery when he publicly denounced slavery from pulpits and platforms across the country. Self-educated, Douglass also published a newspaper in Rochester, New York, from 1847 through 1860 for blacks. He named the paper *The North Star*, because escaping slaves had to follow the North Star to find their way north to freedom.

Fourteenth Amendment

This amendment, ratified in 1868, defined all persons born or naturalized in the United States as citizens. It also stated that the states could not deprive anyone of life, liberty, or property without fair procedures, such as a trial. But even with this amendment, many blacks were still excluded from full citizenship, as were all women.

Freedmen's Villages

Camps established by the federal government toward the end of the Civil War. So many slaves were escaping to the North from Southern plantations that there was nowhere to house them. The government provided housing, as well as food and medical care, for the former slaves.

Fugitive Slave Law

A federal law passed in 1850, requiring that the federal government assist slave owners in getting back their runaway slaves. Federal marshals were ordered to assist slave owners in recapturing slaves and were fined if the slaves escaped from their custody. To ensure the return of all slaves, the law denied slaves any constitutional rights, such as the right to testify at their own trials.

Garrison, William Lloyd (1805-1879)

A champion of the abolitionist movement. Garrison insisted that slavery would end only when the majority of whites experienced a revolution in conscience. Although doing so alienated many of his supporters, Garrison also spoke out strongly for women's rights and pacifism, the belief that using war or violence as a way to resolve conflicts is morally wrong.

itinerant

Traveling from place to place or on a tour, especially to perform some duty or work.

levee

A formal reception or social meeting. This word was often used to refer to formal gatherings with the president or other high officials.

mortgage

A pledge of property to a creditor, such as a bank or individual, commonly to assure payment for a house or other building. The house or building itself is pledged as security to the creditor. If the owner of the property does not pay back the person or institution that lent the money, that person or institution can seize the property.

Phillips, Wendell (1811-1884)

Abolitionist leader and political reformer. A follower of William Lloyd Garrison, he led the struggle for the approval of the Fourteenth and Fifteenth Amendments to the U.S. Constitution. Phillips also argued for giving women the vote, for an end to capital punishment, and for temperance, the complete avoidance of alcohol.

Quakers

The name commonly given to members of the Society of Friends. This religious group believes that something of God exists in everyone and that people can perceive God within themselves. Practicing Quakers work to eliminate human evil as much as possible and to create a nonviolent society. Since they considered slavery a great human evil, many Quakers provided homes for the Underground Railroad.

ratify

To officially approve. Thirty-eight states are now needed to ratify an amendment to the U.S. Constitution.

segregation

The policy and practice of separating races socially, for example, in schools, housing, and industry. *Segregation* refers especially to discriminatory practices against non-whites in a mainly white society. While segregation is now against the law, it continues in many other forms — in the persistence of ghettos where only one race lives, hiring practices that discriminate against particular groups such as blacks, Asians, and women, and in various more subtle separations between people of different races.

Sodom
  According to the Bible, a city in Palestine. God supposedly destroyed Sodom and
  Gomorrah, a nearby city, with a rain of brimstone and fire because the inhabitants of
  these cities behaved so wickedly.

sovereignty
  Supreme and independent political authority. Southern states wanted sovereignty
  over those issues, such as slavery, that they thought affected only their states.

Stanton, Elizabeth Cady (1815-1902)
  A founder of the organized women's rights movement in the United States and a
  strong leader in the struggle to win voting and property rights for women. She, along
  with Susan B. Anthony and Lucretia Mott, formed yearly women's rights conventions.
  At the first convention in 1848, Stanton proposed a resolution that demanded voting
  rights for women for the first time in history. For fifty years, she and Anthony
  collaborated on advocating for various women's issues.

Stowe, Harriet Beecher
  An ardent abolitionist who wrote *Uncle Tom's Cabin* to demonstrate how abusive
  slavery was. Often considered one cause of the Civil War, this best-selling novel
  helped solidify and popularize the antislavery movement in the United States. Stowe
  also wrote poetry, novels, short stories, and several antislavery articles, including
  one about Sojourner Truth.

subjugation
  Literally, "to bring under the yoke." To subjugate someone means to subdue or to
  bring that person under control.

subservience
  Servility. A subservient person submits to the will, guidance, or control of another
  person and behaves in a fawning, menial manner.

Underground Railroad
  A network of "safe houses" that escaping slaves used to travel to free states or to
  Canada. Once in Canada, they could not be prosecuted under the Fugitive Slave Law.
  Organized mainly by Northern blacks, the safe houses provided clothing, shelter, and
  food to the slaves. While many of the slaves escaped independently and made the haz-
  ardous journey across the slave states and to the "railroad," Harriet Tubman, the chief
  organizer of the "railroad," traveled to Southern states and spirited away over 300
  other slaves to freedom.

utopian settlement
  A cooperative community where members try to build a perfect, self-enclosed society. Utopian settlements tried to eliminate political, economic, and social evils. During
  the nineteenth century, many utopian communities were begun but few survived more
  than a few years. Most started by forming small communities where people lived in
  a simple manner, owned all things in common, and shared in the work.

Chronology

1797   Isabella Hardenbergh, nicknamed Belle, is born to slaves Baumfree and Mau-
             Mau Bett on the Hardenbergh family farm in Ulster County, New York.

1799	First New York Emancipation Act is passed, stating that all slaves born after July 4, 1799, would be "free," although males had to serve masters without pay until age twenty-eight. Females had to serve until age twenty-five.
1806	Nine-year-old Belle is sold to John Neely.
1807	Mau-Mau Bett dies.
1808	John Neely sells Belle to Martin Schryver.
1810	Martin Schryver sells Belle to John Dumont.
1814	At seventeen, Belle is forced to marry Thomas, another Dumont slave.
1815	Diana, Belle's first child, is born. In the next ten years, Belle gives birth to Peter, Elizabeth, and Sophia. It is believed that a fourth daughter was born but died in infancy.
1818	The New York state legislature decides that all slaves in New York will be free as of July 4, 1827. Frederick Douglass is born.
1820	After long, heated negotiation, the U.S. Congress approves the Missouri Compromise. This bans slavery in most of the territories gained with the Louisiana Purchase.
1826	Belle takes her freedom and walks away from John Dumont's farm, taking Sophia with her. Diana, Elizabeth, and Peter remain behind.
1827	Belle's son, Peter, is traded to a farmer in Alabama. Belle wins him back.
1829	Belle moves to New York City.
1833	Belle moves to Sing Sing, New York, to be part of The Kingdom, a utopian religious community. The American Anti-Slavery Society is formed in Philadelphia, Pennsylvania.
1839	Peter joins the crew of the whaler *The Zone*. He is believed to have been lost at sea two years later.
1840	The World's Anti-Slavery Convention, meeting in London, England, refuses to seat women delegates.
1843	At forty-six, Belle decides to leave New York City and become a traveling preacher. She takes the name Sojourner Truth. Belle joins the Northampton Association. This group, made up of Quakers, Seventh-Day Adventists, and other Protestant groups, folds in about 1846. Truth then becomes a servant in a household in Northampton for a few years.
1848	**July 19** — The first women's rights convention is held at Seneca Falls, New York. The delegates publish a "Declaration of Sentiments," using the U.S. Declaration of Independence as a model, to point out how women have been excluded from the full benefits of U.S. citizenship.

1849   Truth visits John Dumont for the last time. He admits that slavery is a sin.

1850   In Worcester, Massachusetts, Sojourner attends her first women's rights convention.
Sojourner buys land in Northampton, Massachusetts.
Sojourner publishes her autobiography, the *Narrative of Sojourner Truth*.
The Fugitive Slave Law is passed.

1857   The Supreme Court decides that, despite his having spent time in a free state, Dred Scott remains a slave. The decision means that no African-Americans can ever claim the rights of citizenship. Many Northerners and abolitionists condemn the decision.
Sojourner sells her land in Northampton and buys a house in Harmonia, near Battle Creek, Michigan. Daughters Diana, Elizabeth, and Sophia eventually move nearby.

1859   John Brown attacks the federal arsenal at Harpers Ferry, Virginia, trying to seize weapons for an uprising of slaves. He is captured and hanged.

1861   **February** — Seven Southern states secede from the Union and form the Confederate States of America. In April, four more Southern states secede.
March 4 — Abraham Lincoln takes the oath of the presidency.
April 12 — Confederates fire on Fort Sumter, South Carolina, a federal army base. The Civil War begins.

1863   **January 1** — Union president Lincoln's Emancipation Proclamation goes into effect, freeing slaves in all Confederate states.
July — The U.S. War Department rules that all black troops of any rank are to be paid only the same wage as fugitive slaves who do menial labor.
July 16 — James Caldwell, Sojourner's grandson, is captured by the Confederacy. He is released in 1865. (James is Elizabeth's son by her first husband.)

1864   **October 29** — Truth meets with Lincoln. She is commissioned as a counselor in the freedmen's village in Arlington, Virginia.

1865   The Freedmen's Bureau is established.
Truth is appointed to the Freedmen's Hospital in Washington, D.C.
The Ku Klux Klan is founded in Tennessee to terrorize blacks and prevent them from voting, holding political office, or exercising their new civil rights.
April 9 — Confederate general Robert E. Lee surrenders to Union general Ulysses S. Grant at Appomattox Court House in Virginia.
April 14 — John Wilkes Booth shoots President Lincoln in Ford's Theatre in Washington, D.C. Lincoln dies the next day.
December — The Thirteenth Amendment, which abolishes slavery in all the states, is ratified.

1868   The Fourteenth Amendment is ratified; it grants citizenship to people born or naturalized in the United States but protects only adult males' right to vote.

1870   **March 31** — Sojourner meets with President Ulysses S. Grant.
The Fifteenth Amendment, which guarantees blacks the right to vote, is

ratified. But some states ignore and defy it for decades.

Truth begins lecture tours again, speaking out for women's rights, especially the right to vote, and calling for land in the West to be given to free blacks.

1871   **April 4** — Nannette Gardner, the first woman in the United States to vote, casts her ballot in Detroit, Michigan.

1875   The third edition of Truth's *Narrative* is published and includes the *Book of Life*, letters to Truth and articles about her.

Sammy Banks, Truth's grandson and traveling companion, dies after a long illness. (Sammy is Elizabeth's son by her second husband.)

1876   Truth recovers from an extended illness and attends the Philadelphia Centennial Exposition.

1883   **November 26** — Sojourner Truth dies at home in Battle Creek, Michigan. Daughters Diana and Elizabeth are with her.

1892   Frances Titus commissions artist Frank C. Courter to do a portrait of Sojourner Truth.

1909   The National Association for the Advancement of Colored People (NAACP) is founded to eliminate racism and lynchings.

1916   The Daughters of the American Revolution (DAR) and the first Sojourner Truth Memorial Association join in an effort to erect a marble headstone on Truth's grave.

1942   **February 28** — Riots occur at the Sojourner Truth housing units in Detroit, Michigan, when three African-American families try to move into the project.

1946   A granite tombstone at Sojourner Truth's grave replaces the worn marble one.

1964   The Civil Rights Act of 1964 becomes law. This act prohibits discrimination in employment and in public accommodations, such as restaurants, hotels, and theaters.

1966   The National Organization for Women (NOW) is established to promote the rights of women.

1968   Congress passes the Civil Rights Act of 1968, prohibiting discrimination in housing and real estate sales.

1972   The Equal Rights Amendment (ERA) passes Congress. It states that neither the states nor the federal government may deny or restrict equal rights on account of sex. The required number of states fails to ratify and the proposed amendment expires in 1982.

Index

abolitionism 11-12, 21-30, 34-36, 39, 41, 54, 56, 57, 58
African-American experience 5, 15, 23, 35, 37, 39-46, 49, 54-55

Banks, Sammy 32, 40, 42, 49-50
Battle Creek, Michigan 35, 46, 50, 52

civil rights 6, 47, 54; of blacks 5, 26, 29, 39, 40, 41-43, 44, 47, 48, 52, 54-55, 57-58; of women 5-6, 29-31, 43-47, 52-56, 57
Civil War 5, 26, 32, 34, 35, 37, 38, 39, 40
constitutional amendments 5-6, 41, 43-44, 52, 54

Davis, Jefferson 34, 35
discrimination 40-48, 52-58
Douglass, Frederick 24, 32, 34, 49, 51, 52, 58
Dumont, John 8-10, 12-14, 58

Emancipation Proclamation 5, 35, 41

Fowler, Eliza 23-24
Freedmen's Bureau 39-40
freedmen's villages 39

Gandhi, Mohandas (Mahatma) 56-58
Garrison, William Lloyd 24, 29, 43, 58
Gedney, Solomon 14-16, 18, 23
Grant, Ulysses S. 40, 47-48

Jim Crow laws 42, 44, 55
Johnson, Andrew 40

King, Martin Luther, Jr. 56-58
Ku Klux Klan 42

Lincoln, Abraham 34, 35, 38, 39, 40, 44, 48

Narrative of Sojourner Truth 32, 38, 52
National Association for the Advancement of Colored People (NAACP) 54-55
National Organization for Women (NOW) 55-56
Neely, John 7-8
New York City 16, 18-20
nonviolence 23-24, 56-58
Northampton Association 21, 24-25, 29, 32

Pierson, Elijah 16-17
poll taxes 52, 54

Quakers 12, 13, 57

Schryver, Martin 8
Scott, Dred 25-26
slavery 5-16, 23, 25-26, 35-36, 39, 41, 46
Stanton, Elizabeth Cady 29, 43
Stowe, Harriet Beecher 48-49
Student Nonviolent Coordinating Committee (SNCC) 58

Truth, Sojourner
    and abolitionism 12, 21-28, 30-31, 34, 36, 38, 49
    appearance of 4, 5, 26, 27, 36
    birth and childhood of 6-9
    children of 10, 16, 19, 21, 28; Peter 10, 14-16, 18-19, 21, 23; Sophia 12, 16
    and Civil War 35
    courtship and marriage 9-10, 21
    and Dumont family 9, 10, 12-16, 39
    employment of 16, 18, 19, 21, 35, 39, 40, 42
    and Hardenbergh family 7-8, 10
    health of 44-45, 48-51
    homes of 31, 35, 50
    and The Kingdom 16-18, 27
    legacy of 25, 52, 54-58
    legal battles of 15-16, 17-18, 43
    and nonviolence 23-24, 56-58
    parents of 6-8, 10-11, 40, 44
    reactions to 24, 26-28, 32, 36, 48, 51-52, 58
    religious background and speeches of 6, 7, 9, 12-14, 17, 19, 20-21, 24, 25, 29-30, 47, 51
    and rights of freed slaves 39, 41-44, 47-48
    and street railroad 5, 42-43
    travels of 21, 26, 29, 38, 39, 49, 58
    and western lands 47-50
    and women's rights 29-31, 38, 43-44, 45-47, 48, 49, 50, 54-58

Van Wagener, Isaac and Maria 12-13, 16

women's rights movement 8, 29-31, 43-44, 46-47, 52-58